"How about a confession?"

"I'm listening," he assured her.

"This is the first time I've ever danced in a field of cows."

"The cows are on the other side of the fence, so we're actually dancing in a field beside a field of cows."

"I stand corrected," she said. "In a field *beside* a field of cows."

He smiled then. "And if I kissed you now, would it be the first time you've ever been kissed in a field beside a field of cows?"

Her breath caught in her throat, but somehow she managed to respond, "It would be."

"Then let's make this a night of firsts," he said and lowered his mouth to touch hers.

And then—

Oh. My. God.

—he *was* kissing her.

His lips were warm and firm and confident as they moved over hers, proving that the man had not just experience but some serious skill, and Haylee's brain scrambled as she tried to keep up.

She'd been kissed before, of course, but never like this.

MATCH MADE IN HAVEN:
Where gold rush meets gold bands

Dear Reader,

I've always loved how the world seems to transform in winter. It's not just the holiday lights that I see around the neighborhood or the classic carols that I hear in all the stores. It's the contrast of a clear blue sky against a blanket of fresh snow, marked only by the tracks of the rabbits who live under our evergreen trees—at least until we let our rescued chocolate Lab out to play! But mostly it's the sense of joy and wonder that never fails to fill our hearts and makes us believe in the possibility of peace on earth and goodwill toward all others...

Christmas has always been my favorite time of the year, and I'm even more excited about this festive season because I have a Haven romance to share with you! The northern Nevada town does the holidays in style, with evergreen wreaths hanging from the lampposts on Main Street, playful holiday scenes painted on the storefront windows and multicolored lights illuminating the big tree in front of Town Hall.

And while the temperatures might be frigid, the gossip is hotter than ever. The biggest story in town? Haylee Gilmore is going to have Trevor Blake's babies. That's right—she's pregnant with twins!

Both expectant parents have reasons to be wary when it comes to matters of the heart, but perhaps a Christmas miracle will make them see that happily-ever-after is possible.

I hope you enjoy this visit to Haven, and Haylee and Trevor's story. And please come back in the spring for Mitchell Gilmore's long-awaited reunion with his first love (and now mom of two) Kelsey Delgado.

Happy reading and happy holidays!

Brenda Harlen

Meet Me Under the Mistletoe

BRENDA HARLEN

HARLEQUIN
SPECIAL
EDITION

ISBN-13: 978-1-335-89491-5

Meet Me Under the Mistletoe

Copyright © 2020 by Brenda Harlen

Recycling programs
for this product may
not exist in your area.

Harlequin Enterprises ULC
22 Adelaide St. West, 40th Floor
Toronto, Ontario M5H 4E3, Canada
www.Harlequin.com

Printed in U.S.A.

Brenda Harlen is a former attorney who once had the privilege of appearing before the Supreme Court of Canada. The practice of law taught her a lot about the world and reinforced her determination to become a writer—because in fiction, she could promise a happy ending! Now she is an award-winning, RITA® Award—nominated nationally bestselling author of more than thirty titles for Harlequin. You can keep up-to-date with Brenda on Facebook and Twitter, or through her website, brendaharlen.com.

Books by Brenda Harlen

Harlequin Special Edition

Match Made in Haven

The Sheriff's Nine-Month Surprise
Her Seven-Day Fiancé
Six Weeks to Catch a Cowboy
Claiming the Cowboy's Heart
Double Duty for the Cowboy
One Night with the Cowboy

Montana Mavericks: Six Brides for Six Brothers

Maverick Christmas Surprise

Montana Mavericks: The Lonelyhearts Ranch

Bring Me a Maverick for Christmas!

Montana Mavericks: The Great Family Roundup

The Maverick's Midnight Proposal

Visit the Author Profile page
at Harlequin.com for more titles.

This book is dedicated to readers everywhere.

Over the past year, there have been far too many headlines and hashtags that made me (and likely everyone else!) feel as if the world had been turned upside down and was spinning out of control. Too many days when I wondered what was the point of sitting down at the computer to write.

Then came the social media posts from readers asking for more stories—because they wanted happy endings. They wanted hope.

Or, at the very least, they wanted to escape from the real world for a few hours.

I hope this story does that for you.

Chapter One

Haylee Gilmore kicked aside her work boots as she hung her coveralls on the hook beside the door, aware that her roommate, who also happened to be her sister, would curse a blue streak if she tripped over them. Finley's shoes, half a dozen pairs of three-inch heels in various styles and colors—and not even a fraction of the number to be found in her bedroom closet, were neatly lined up beneath the deacon's bench on the other side of the door.

"Fin? Are you home?"

"In the kitchen."

Haylee followed her voice—and the mouthwatering scents of tomato and basil—to the kitchen.

When the sisters decided to move out of their parents' Victorian home and into the carriage house apartment together, they agreed to divide the domestic chores equally, alternating cooking duties and sharing the housecleaning and laundry responsibilities. But it was quickly apparent to both that Finley was the much better cook (though Haylee was indisputably the master of baking), so now the younger sister spent more time in the kitchen and less scrubbing toilets.

"Something smells good," Haylee noted.

"I'm making deconstructed lasagna."

Apparently Finley had been listening when Haylee grumbled the night before that it would be nice to eat something other than raw vegetables every once in a while. Yes, it was early June and salad was refreshing, but it wasn't, in her opinion, a meal—even when her sister dressed it up with nuts and berries.

Lasagna was a meal.

Opening the refrigerator to snag a can of Coke, she asked, "Do you want one?"

Finley made a face. "You know I only drink diet."

"Fake sugar isn't good for you," Haylee said, even as she returned to the fridge to grab a can of diet cola for her sister.

"I know." Finley took the proffered can and popped the tab. "But real sugar won't help me squeeze into the Donna Karan dress I'm wearing for the Krieghoff wedding Friday night."

"You'll look fabulous no matter what you wear."

"Says the sister who could wear anything and yet chooses to live in jeans and T-shirts."

"Jeans and T-shirts are comfortable," Haylee pointed out in her own defense. "Not to mention appropriate for my job."

"For your job," Finley agreed. "But there's more to life than work—or there should be."

It was a familiar topic of conversation between them, because Finley was social and outgoing and, despite living with Haylee for her whole life, couldn't understand that her older-by-eleven-months sister was not.

Haylee ignored the comment and lowered herself into a seat at the table to riffle through the mail. She paused when she found a thick envelope with her name and address handwritten in fancy script. "What's this?"

Finley glanced over as she mixed ricotta in with the meat, noodles and sauce already in the skillet. "An invitation to Caleb and Brielle's wedding. I got one, too."

Caleb was a paternal cousin who lived in Haven, Nevada—along with most of the rest of the Gilmore family—and Brielle was the girl he'd been in love with since high school—and had apparently eloped with not long after their high school graduation eight years earlier.

"I thought they were already married," Haylee remarked, sliding a finger under the flap to open the envelope.

"They are, but they never actually had a wedding, so Brielle's grandfather is hosting a big reception to make things more official, show off their new baby and prove that the feud is over."

Haylee swallowed another mouthful of Coke. Though their father had left Haven, Nevada, some forty years earlier, he'd told his children about the Gilmore-Blake feud that dated back more than one hundred and fifty years to when Everett Gilmore, his great-great grandfather, discovered that the exact parcel of land he'd bought had also been sold to a man by the name of Samuel Blake. Rather than risk taking the matter to court and having one of them end up with nothing, the two men had decided to split the property down the middle, using Eighteen-Mile Creek—or Crooked Creek, as it was referred to by the locals—as the east and west dividing line between the two ranches.

Because the Gilmores had already started to build their home in the valley—on the west side of the creek, the Blakes were relegated to the higher elevation on the east—where the land was mostly comprised of rocky hills and ridges. The Gilmores' cattle immediately benefited from grazing on more hospitable terrain, while the Blakes struggled for a lot of years to keep their herd viable—until silver and gold were found in the hills on their side of the creek and they gave up ranching in favor of mining.

In addition, there was an ill-fated love affair between Everett Gilmore's daughter, Maggie, and Samuel Blake's youngest son, James, that ended with a stillborn child and further soured the relationship between the two families.

Haylee pulled the invitation out of the envelope and skimmed the details. "The wedding's in less than three weeks."

"A surefire way to keep the guest list down," Finley remarked, "is to wait until people have other plans to invite them."

"Obviously you have other plans," she noted.

"I'm an event planner—I always have other plans."

"And yet, you still manage to have a social life."

"You could have one, too, if you wanted one," her sister said.

It was true that Haylee had never worried too much about filling her after-work and weekend hours with parties and events. She was mostly content with her own company—and even happier with a good book in hand. It was enough for her to get together with a friend for lunch or meet a coworker for drinks every now and again. And for several years, that had been her routine. But over the past few months, she'd noticed an unsettling trend beginning to disrupt her comfortable routine.

Starting with Lisa, who'd had to reschedule their lunch date three times in order to squeeze it in between dress fittings and cake tastings and other appointments in preparation for her upcoming wedding; followed by Candace, who'd bailed on drinks one weekend because she hadn't been feeling well—and then confided that drinks would be out for the foreseeable future because she was pregnant; and, most recently, by Nancy, who'd simply been a no-show for Sunday brunch because her boyfriend had surprised her with a weekend getaway to Lake Tahoe, and she'd been so excited about the trip she hadn't thought to even send a quick text message to Haylee about the change of plans.

Haylee was sincerely happy for her friends, but she was also suddenly aware of the emptiness of her own life. Especially in light of the fact that get-togethers with Josslin had already dropped off her calendar because the first-time mom was understandably preoccupied with her new baby.

"It might be fun to catch up with the Haven relatives," she said now, thinking specifically of her cousin

Katelyn—an attorney married to the sheriff and mother to an adorable toddler—and Katelyn's sister, Skylar—who worked as a counselor with at-risk kids and tended bar at the local watering hole.

"It might be," Finley agreed.

"Do you know if Dad and Colleen are going to the wedding?"

"I doubt it, especially considering that they've already committed to making the trip at the end of August for Grandma and Grandpa's sixtieth anniversary."

"What about Logan?" she asked, naming their younger brother, a junior architect at a local firm.

Finley shook her head. "I called him yesterday, hoping to snag him as a plus-one for a recently jilted bridesmaid in the Krieghoff wedding party, but he said he's going to be working around the clock until the end of the month on a major design project."

"Well, I'm not going by myself," Haylee decided, tossing the invitation aside.

"Why not?" Finley scooped pasta into two bowls.

"Because I'd feel pathetic."

"More pathetic than sitting home alone?" her sister asked, not unkindly.

Haylee pushed away from the table to get cutlery and napkins. "I won't be alone. I'll be with Simon."

"Giving him a man's name doesn't change the fact that he's a cat—and if hanging out with your cat is the extent of your plans, that *is* pathetic."

"I know," she admitted.

And the truth was, she'd gone to the local SPCA and adopted Simon because, after numerous unsuccessful—and perhaps half-hearted—efforts to find companionship through online dating, she'd finally given up and acknowledged that if she didn't want to be alone, she was going to have to get a pet.

Finley sat at the table, across from her sister, and pulled her cell phone out of her pocket. "What's the email address on the invitation? I want to RSVP before I forget."

Her sister's thumbs flew over the keypad as Haylee read out the requested information.

"Thanks." Finley set her phone beside her can of soda. "Now Patrick at the Silver Star Vacation Ranch knows that I cannot attend, but my sister Haylee is very much looking forward to the event."

"What? You didn't—"

"I did," Finley confirmed, picking up her fork.

"But I never said I would go," she protested.

"No, you didn't," her sister agreed. "But I don't want you spending another Saturday night alone at home."

Haylee sighed. "Can I take Simon as my plus-one?"

"No." Finley pushed her noodles around in her bowl. "You're going to go with a mind open to the possibility that you might actually meet somebody."

"In Haven, Nevada?" She scooped up a forkful of pasta. "A town of…what? Maybe two hundred people?"

Finley tapped the screen of her phone again, performing a quick Google search. "Twenty-two hundred."

"Because I can't find a man in a city of half a million, but Mr. Right is going to be waiting for me in a town of twenty-two hundred," she remarked dryly.

"I don't expect you to find Mr. Right at the wedding—although Mr. Right *Now* would be a good start," her sister said with a wink.

Haylee sighed again. "I guess I'd better look into flights."

Because she had no intention of driving for seven hours in each direction when she was only going for a weekend.

"And hotels."

Was there even a hotel in Haven?

She thought she remembered hearing something about her cousin Liam renovating an old inn in town and made a mental note to look it up…after dinner. Because she'd worked through lunch and was starving.

"And you're going to need something to wear," Finley said.

"I'm sure I've got something in my closet that will work."

"I'm sure you don't," her sister countered. "Even a country wedding requires something dressier than steel-toed boots and a hard hat."

"How about Converse high-tops and a baseball cap?" she asked, joking.

Mostly.

Finley shook her head despairingly. "There are times when I sincerely question how we're related."

There were times when Haylee wondered the same thing.

And because there was no denying that her sister had much better fashion sense than Haylee, she swallowed her pride and said, "Will you go shopping with me?"

Now Finley grinned. "I thought you'd never ask."

Of course, it wasn't enough for her sister to ensure that Haylee had a new dress for the occasion. Finley had insisted that she also needed new shoes to go with the new dress, a purse to match the shoes and suitable undergarments to wear under the dress.

Now Haylee was standing in front of the mirror of her ground floor room at the Stagecoach Inn—the local boutique hotel indeed owned by her cousin Liam and managed by his wife, Macy—wearing a tiny pair of pink bikini panties and a matching lace bra that she had to concede was nothing less than an engineering marvel, as the garment somehow lifted and enhanced her body in a way that made it appear as if she actually had breasts.

Maybe Finley was right, she acknowledged, as she wiggled into the simple sheath-style dress in a pale shade of peachy-pink that her sister had called "coral." Maybe she'd never felt sexy because plain cotton wasn't sexy.

Or maybe she was deluding herself into thinking that some pretty clothes and pricey makeup could turn her into a different woman—a *confident* woman.

You've always been beautiful, even if you've never seen yourself that way, Finley had said. *But this outfit should give you a better understanding of the power that goes hand in hand with being a woman.*

With her sister's words echoing in her head, Haylee smoothed the front of her dress and reassessed.

Beautiful was a stretch, she decided.

On the other hand, she wasn't *un*attractive.

The sweep of mascara on her lashes made them look longer and thicker—and she didn't think anyone would guess that she'd needed three Q-tips to clean up around her eyes because putting mascara on her own lashes was a lot more challenging than letting Finley do it. The bronzer on her cheekbones added definition and just a hint of color, and the peach-colored gloss on her lips made them shine.

Peering into the mirror, she thought the overall result was pretty close to the transformation Finley had effected.

So much so that Haylee doubted any of her coworkers would recognize her if they saw her now.

She slid her feet into the high-heeled sandals her sister had insisted were perfect for the dress, then picked up the wristlet that coordinated with the shoes and would hold her ID and keys (and the single condom that she'd tucked inside, because even if she was skeptical about her odds of meeting someone, she didn't believe in taking chances). Honestly, Haylee had spent more money during that one shopping trip with her sister than she usually spent on clothes in a year—which Finley assured her was *not* something she should be proud of—and that was before they'd hit the cosmetics department at Saks.

Trust me, it will all be worthwhile, Finley had promised.

So Haylee took a few cautious turns around her hotel room, practicing so that she'd be steady on her feet. The skinny heels did take some getting used to, but she figured she'd be okay as long as she didn't overindulge.

Although Haven didn't have an actual taxi service and Uber hadn't yet found its way to the town, Jesse Blake had hired a couple drivers so that none of the wedding guests would need to worry about transportation to and from the event, especially if they had a few drinks. The exaggerated wolf whistle of the driver who came for Haylee was more flattering than offensive—but maybe that was because the man was seventy years old if he was a day. Still, his reaction bolstered her confidence a little more and his steady chatter on the drive to the Silver Star helped loosen the knots of trepidation in her belly.

She arrived just as the guests were being ushered toward an outdoor seating area facing a gazebo decorated with vines and flowers. Haylee slipped into a vacant seat at the back and watched through misty eyes as Brielle and Caleb walked down the aisle hand in hand.

The bride wore a floor-length vintage lace wedding dress with cap sleeves, a wreath of flowers on her head and cowboy boots on her feet. Her groom was in a Western-style tux complete with cowboy hat and boots. As they renewed their vows in front of their families and friends—including their adorable infant son—there was no doubt in Haylee's mind that love had finally triumphed over the age-old feud between their respective families.

After the ceremony, she made her way through the crowd, stopping to chat with various relatives along the way, assuring her grandparents—who expressed pleasure at seeing Haylee but disappointment that her siblings and parents weren't in attendance—that the whole family would be making the trip in August for Jack and Evelyn's big anniversary party, and snapping photos of the decorations with her iPhone to share with her sister, who was always eager for new ideas that she might incorporate into her own events.

Everywhere Haylee looked, there were barrels and

buckets overflowing with greenery and white blooms. Fence rails had been draped with evergreen boughs trimmed with satin bows. Bistro lights were strung above the temporary dance floor, and the nearby food tent was filled with long tables heavy under the weight of hot and cold food servers, layered trays of sweets and cookies, a champagne fountain, kegs of beer, and coolers filled with sodas and juice pouches.

She lifted a glass of champagne from the tray of a passing waiter and sipped the cool, bubbly liquid as she made her way back outside again. Her gaze moved through the crowd, searching for someone—anyone— to talk to so she didn't look like the complete wallflower that she was.

Still, she was surprised when she caught the eye of a guy near the entrance of the tent—a guy so hot that her heart actually skipped a beat.

The chinos and button-down shirt he wore were appropriate for a country wedding; the cowboy hat and boots emphasized the country part. She guessed his height to be over six feet, though it was hard to be certain at a distance. Shaded somewhat by the brim of his Stetson were dark eyes, a narrow nose and perfectly shaped lips that, even as she watched, curved into a slow smile.

It was the kind of smile that a guy bestowed upon a girl to express his interest. Just because Haylee couldn't ever recall being the recipient of such a smile didn't prevent her from recognizing its meaning, and she wondered, with a small tug of envy, which lucky girl in the crowd was the subject of his attention.

Then her gaze lifted to his again—and she found his eyes focused on *her*!

No way, she decided, locking knees that had gone weak at the mere possibility. He had to be looking at someone else, someone standing close by or even behind her.

Usually that *someone* was Finley, but her sister was at home in Oakland, so Haylee turned her head to look. But her back was against the split-rail fence, and there was no one else around.

Which meant that he was looking *at her*.

Smiling *at her*.

And so she did what any self-respecting, socially inept girl would do when confronted by the attention of an incredibly hot guy.

She fled.

Chapter Two

Trevor Blake knew that inviting a woman to attend any kind of family event might give her the impression that their relationship meant something more than it really did, and inviting a woman to be his plus-one for a wedding seemed to imply that he was open to the possibility of a wedding in their future. So he'd decided that bringing a date to a family wedding seemed like a Very Bad Idea and resigned himself to attending Brielle and Caleb's reception on his own.

He'd had more than a few opportunities to second-guess his decision before the vows were even exchanged, as his solo attendance resulted in him being subjected to pitying glances and sympathetic slaps on the shoulder—not to mention the unwelcome and misguided matchmaking efforts of various aunts and cousins. But then he'd spotted the sexy brunette in the pink dress.

She'd disappeared into the crowd immediately after the nuptials, and he was scrutinizing the gathering, trying to catch another glimpse of her, when his brother joined him.

"I should've brought a date," Devin said, offering him one of the two glasses he carried.

Trevor swallowed a mouthful of beer before responding. "Has Aunt Millie offered to set you up with her bridge partner's granddaughter yet?"

"It was her bridge partner's second husband's granddaughter," Devin clarified.

"Oh, well, in that case," Trevor said, as he casually scanned the crowd again.

Apparently not casually enough, as his brother asked, "You looking for anyone in particular?"

"No," he lied.

"You once told me that weddings were a great place to meet single girls, but everyone seems to be paired up," Devin remarked, sounding disappointed.

"Not everyone," Trevor said. "Check out the one in the short green dress talking to Brielle right now—isn't that one of her roommates from New York?"

His brother nodded. "That's Grace. Lily's the one in the flowered sundress."

"Well, I'd put money on Grace being single and interested, because she's been sending furtive glances in your direction all afternoon."

"Really?" Devin asked.

"Really," Trevor confirmed.

Then his brother shook his head. "New York's a long

way away and I'm not interested in a long-distance relationship."

"Who said anything about a relationship?" he countered. "Why can't you just enjoy the company of an attractive female for a few hours?"

"Are you really so opposed to the possibility of falling in love again?" Devin asked, sounding worried.

"Love isn't all hearts and flowers," Trevor told him. "It's just the transitional stage between infatuation and heartbreak."

"And yet, despite that cynical perspective, you never have any trouble getting a date when you want one."

"I'm a Blake," he said, a simple statement of fact. "And so are you, so why don't you go on over there and ask Grace to dance?"

"Maybe later," Devin said, lifting his glass to indicate that he still had a drink to finish.

But Trevor knew the beer in his brother's hand was only an excuse. Devin was a whiz when it came to anything to do with computers, but he didn't have the first clue about how to interact with the female gender. He managed to hold his own with family members or work colleagues, but when it came to anyone with whom he experienced even a hint of a spark of attraction, his brilliant brother turned into a babbling idiot.

"Later might be too late," he felt compelled to warn. "Because Mitchell Gilmore looks like he's getting ready to make a move."

Devin frowned as he watched the other man make his way toward Grace, then his frown turned into a wince. "Don't look now, but Aunt Millie's heading in this direction."

Trevor heeded the warning, but mostly because his attention had been snagged by a flash of pink.

And there she was again—standing in front of the fence of a nearby paddock, sipping from a flute of champagne.

He would have bet his annual dividends that she was an out-of-town guest, because if she'd been a local resident, he would have met her long before now. He would have made a point of it.

She was on the skinny side of slender, and though he was generally attracted to a woman with more distinct curves, there was something about her that immediately appealed to him. She had dark hair tied up in some kind of twist that made him want to let it loose to tumble over her shoulders, to feel its softness in his hands. And she had long, shapely legs that he could easily imagine—

She caught him looking at him then, and her eyes went wide, as if she was privy to his innermost thoughts. Or maybe she was simply surprised by his blatant perusal.

He smiled, to assure her that he meant no offense by his attention, and waited for her to smile back—an acceptance of his wordless invitation.

Instead she turned her head, breaking the connection and snapping the thread of tension that had stretched between them across the distance, set her empty glass on top of a nearby barrel and walked away.

With a shrug, Trevor resumed his survey of the crowd.

There were plenty of other females in attendance, and he was certain he could find someone to flirt and dance with, if that's what he wanted.

But it was the one in pink who intrigued him.

And it had been a long time since anyone had done so.

He handed his half-empty glass to his brother. "Excuse me," he said. "There's someone I need to talk to."

Devin, following the direction of his gaze, asked, "Who is she?"

"I don't know, but I'm going to find out," Trevor vowed.

This was why she didn't wear fancy shoes, Haylee acknowledged, as she carefully made her way across the uneven ground. Sure, the sandals looked good with the dress, but they were more suited to a polished floor than country fields.

The skyscraper heels were out of place here, just like Haylee. And as she moved farther away from the gathering, she almost felt like a little girl again, playing dress up with her sister, pretending to be somebody that she wasn't.

At the end of the day, she knew the external trappings didn't matter. What mattered was the person inside—and that person didn't have the first clue about the rules of the games men and women played. But as she walked away from the smiling stranger, for the first time in her adult life Haylee found herself sincerely regretting that lack of knowledge and experience.

Just be yourself, Finley had urged. *Making conversation with a guy is no different than making conversation with anyone else.*

Haylee *knew* that, of course, because she talked to guys every day.

In fact, Monday through Friday, she spent more time in the company of men than women. But that was on the job and most of those guys were her coworkers. It wasn't easy for a female electrician to be accepted in what was predominantly still a male occupation, and it had taken some time—and a lot of hard work—to earn the respect and trust of her colleagues. The fact that they talked with their mouths full, didn't bother to censor their language and occasionally offered to buy her a beer after work proved that she'd done so. That, to them, she was just one of the guys. Certainly none of them had ever looked at her the way the gorgeous guy standing outside the food tent had looked at her.

Of course, he wasn't seeing the real Haylee Gilmore but rather the image that her sister had helped her create, to give her the confidence to put herself out there and meet new people. Finley would be so disappointed to know that her sister had run away from the first guy who'd made eye contact with her.

So focused was Haylee on her internal recriminations that she didn't notice the hole in the ground until she'd stepped in it. She immediately teetered, her arms windmilling as she fought to regain her balance. But it was no use—her heel was stuck and the rest of her was about to get up close and personal with the ground.

In fact, she had just about half a second to wonder if she'd ever be able to get the inevitable dirt and grass stains out of her dress before a pair of strong arms caught her.

"Oh," she said, breathless not from the stumble but the catch—and that was before she recognized the guy who'd done the catching.

"Are you okay?" he asked.

Of course, his voice was as perfect as the rest of him, and all her girl parts quivered in response to the sexy timbre.

"Um, yeah. I think so."

"Gopher hole," he told her, bending to retrieve the shoe that was still lodged in the ground. "A local hazard."

"I think the shoes are the hazard," she admitted.

"Maybe," he acknowledged, holding the sandal so that she could slide her foot back into it. "But they sure do look good on you."

He lifted the back strap over her heel, the pad of his thumb brushing against her skin, an unexpectedly sensual caress that raised goose bumps on her arms. Then he adjusted the straps that crossed over the top of her foot, to ensure they weren't twisted, and rubbed a spot of dirt off her shiny pink toenail.

"Nice color."

And she said a silent prayer of thanks to her sister for bullying her into a pedicure at the end of their marathon shopping session.

"Thanks," she said. "And for the rescue."

"It's what I do," he said as he straightened up again.

He topped her height by a good two or three inches, even with Haylee wearing heels, confirming that her original estimate of his height had been accurate. But his masculine good looks were even more potent at close range.

Making conversation with a guy is no different than making conversation with anyone else.

Finley was right—she *could* do this.

She *would* do this.

"Professional knight in shining armor?" she queried lightly.

"Strictly amateur," he said with a wink.

And her heart skipped again.

Damn he was potent.

But look at that, she mused. In a town of twenty-two hundred people, at a wedding with a significantly lesser number of guests in attendance, she was having a conversation—some might even say bantering—with a good-looking guy.

A *really good-looking guy.*

"So…are you a friend of the bride or groom?" he asked her now.

"Actually, I'm a cousin of the groom." She proffered her hand. "Haylee Gilmore."

He took her hand, but instead of shaking it, simply held it in his own. "No kidding," he said, sounding amused. "I'm a cousin of the bride."

"Do you have a name, cousin of the bride?"

"Trevor Blake."

"It's nice to meet you, Trevor Blake."

"The pleasure is mine, Haylee Gilmore."

She managed a smile and resisted the urge to press a hand to her stomach, where butterflies were fluttering just because she was standing close to him.

So close she could smell his aftershave—or maybe it was his soap. Either way, the scent clouded her brain, far more potent than the single glass of champagne she'd drunk.

"So where are you from, Haylee Gilmore? Because I know you're not from around here."

"Oakland, California."

"You must be close to your cousin, to have traveled so far to celebrate his wedding."

"Truthfully, I haven't seen Caleb—or any of my Haven cousins—in years," she confided. "This wedding was a good excuse to do just that."

"Did your boyfriend make the trip with you?"

Boyfriend?

She almost laughed out loud at the question, but of course that would ruin the image she was trying to project—apparently with some success, as this guy believed there might be someone with her. Or waiting for her back home.

Instead, she shook her head. "No boyfriend." And then, because the opening was too perfect to resist, she asked, "How about you?"

He shook his head. "Nope—no boyfriend."

She could feel the heat climb into her cheeks.

Then he grinned. "And no girlfriend, either."

"That's good," she said, and her face burned hotter. "I mean—"

He chuckled, saving her the effort of trying to fumble for the right words—or any words that didn't make her sound even more awkward and inept.

"It is good," he said. "Because it means there's no one to object if I ask you to dance."

She glanced back at the reception area and the mass of bodies crowded together on the dance floor.

"Are you asking me to dance?" she queried.

"I am," he confirmed and, without waiting for a response, drew her into his arms.

"Wait…you want to dance right here?"

"We can hear the music well enough, can't we?" he asked, swaying to the slow beat of Sam Smith's "Stay With Me."

The music wasn't very loud, but it was audible, and her body was already falling under the seductive spell of his movements.

"And by the time we made our way to the dance floor, this song would be over, likely to be followed by something like 'Twist and Shout' to get the crowd bouncing around again."

"You don't like 'Twist and Shout'?"

"It's a great song," he said. "But not one that would be conducive to me holding you—and I really wanted to hold you."

"It wasn't enough that I already fell into your arms—literally?"

"No." He held her gaze for a long moment. "It wasn't enough."

She could feel herself falling again—under his spell, this time, melting against him.

But how could she be expected to resist a guy who was as charming as he was good-looking?

And why should she even try?

What was wrong with indulging her own desires just a little, for just this one night?

"Tell me about yourself," he suggested, as they continued to dance under the stars. "What do you do in Oakland, California?"

One more piece of advice, Finley had said, as Haylee was zipping up her suitcase, ready to head out the door. *Don't talk about your job.*

Why not?

Because some guys are intimidated by a woman who wears a tool belt to work.

I wouldn't want to be with a guy who can't respect what I do.

Of course you wouldn't, her sister agreed. *But you're not looking for a life partner this weekend, just someone with whom to practice your flirting skills. And maybe your kissing skills.* Finley grinned then. *And maybe more.*

"I work for an electrical contracting company," Haylee finally said, in answer to his question. "What do you do?"

"I work for a local mining company."

"So you're not really a cowboy?" she asked, only the teensiest bit disappointed.

"Occasionally on weekends, I help out at the family ranch," he said, then winked. "But women really dig the hat."

She couldn't deny it was true. "And this local mining company…that would be Blake Mining?" she surmised. "The hugely successful silver and gold excavator that is Haven's single biggest employer and, I'd guess from your name, a family business?"

"And now that all my secrets have been revealed, you have to tell me something else about you," he said.

"Hmm…" She paused, as if considering what to reveal. The problem was, her life really wasn't very interesting. "How about a confession?"

"I'm listening," he assured her.

"This is the first time I've ever danced in a field of cows."

"The cows are on the other side of the fence, so we're actually dancing in a field beside a field of cows."

"I stand corrected," she said. "This is the first time I've ever danced in a field *beside* a field of cows."

He smiled then. "And if I kissed you now, would it be the first time you've ever been kissed in a field beside a field of cows?"

Her breath caught in her throat, but somehow she managed to respond. "It would be."

"Then let's make this a night of firsts," he said, and tipped the brim of his hat up before lowering his mouth to touch hers.

And then—

Oh.

My.

God.

—he *was* kissing her.

His lips were warm and firm and confident as they moved over hers, proving that he had not just experience but some serious skill, and Haylee's brain scrambled as she tried to keep up.

She'd been kissed before, of course, but never like this.

No one had ever made her feel so much—*want* so much—with just a kiss. When his tongue slid between her lips, her brain stopped trying to keep up and simply shut down, letting her instincts take over.

She lifted her hands to his shoulders, holding on to him for support as the ground seemed to shift beneath her feet. His hands skimmed up her back, not touching so much as teasing, stoking her desire, making her burn with want, with need. She pressed closer to him, marveling at his hardness, melting into his heat, word-lessly asking for more and offering everything that she had to give.

It was Trevor who finally ended the kiss, easing his mouth from hers only when they were both breathless.

"You are a dangerous woman, Haylee Gilmore," he said, whispering the words against her lips.

Dangerous?

He obviously didn't know her at all.

Or maybe she'd underestimated herself for a lot of years, because when she was with Trevor, she felt different.

Stronger. Sexier. Bolder.

And, if not dangerous, at least a little reckless.

"You started it," she reminded him.

"Yeah," he acknowledged. "And I was close to finishing it, too, in a field beside a field of cows."

The idea was more appealing than she wanted to admit. "That would have been another first for me," she said lightly.

"Me, too." He brushed his thumb over her bottom lip, still tingling from his kiss. "We should probably get back to the party."

"Okay," she agreed.

But he didn't step away from her. Not yet.

"How long are you going to be in town?" he asked instead.

"I have an early flight back to Oakland in the morning."

"That's not very long at all," he noted, sounding sincerely disappointed by this revelation. "I was hoping we could spend the day together and get to know one another a little better."

And then some kind of primal instinct took over, causing Haylee to throw caution—and common sense—to the wind. "Why don't we spend the night together instead?"

Chapter Three

Trevor lifted his bottle of beer to his lips, his gaze focused on the baseball game on the enormous television that covered most of one wall in the living room of his brother's town house. He enjoyed watching a good game, but this wasn't one—the Oakland A's were trailing the Houston Astros by several runs, and it was only the top of the fourth inning.

He swallowed another mouthful of beer as the batter connected with the next pitch and sent it flying over the right field fence, adding three more runs to the Astros' score.

"We should try to get to a game sometime soon," Trevor remarked, as the A's manager finally jogged to the mound and signaled a pitching change.

"I'm always up for a road trip," Devin readily agreed.

Trevor pulled his phone out of his pocket and tapped on the screen. "The A's are at home against the Rangers in a couple weeks."

His brother reached for the tablet on the coffee table in front of him and opened the calendar app. "I've got a conference in Montreal that weekend."

Trevor scrolled through the Athletics' schedule. "Two weeks after that, they're playing the Mets."

Devin wrinkled his nose. "Here's a better idea," he suggested as an alternative. "We fly to New York to see the Yankees."

"That wouldn't really be a road trip now, would it?"

"It could be, if we drove to New York."

"We're not driving to New York," Trevor told him.

"Yeah, considering how distracted you've been the last couple of weeks, that's probably not a good idea."

"I haven't been distracted," he denied. "I've just had a lot on my mind."

"A lot?" Devin echoed dubiously. "Or a woman?"

Trevor scowled.

"I was at the wedding," his brother reminded him. "I saw you dancing with that girl only a short while before both of you disappeared from the reception."

"So?"

"So it seems to me that you've been distracted since that night. What's the matter? Did you strike out?"

"No, I didn't strike out."

"But you didn't get very far," Devin surmised. "I'm guessing a single...maybe a double."

"I can't believe you're still using baseball analogies to describe sex."

"Baseball is timeless," his brother insisted. "Also, it seemed apropos to our original topic of conversation."

"Apropos, huh?"

"And you're deflecting," Devin noted.

"I'm not deflecting."

"Then tell me what happened with Haylee Gilmore."

Trevor lifted his brows, a silent question.

His brother shrugged. "I might have asked someone who she was when I saw you leave with her. And then I Googled her."

"Why?" he asked.

"Because you're my brother and I wanted to be sure you weren't being targeted—again—by a wannabe social media influencer who thought she could increase her number of followers by posting photos with hashtag Blake Mining Heir."

He frowned, not just at the possibility but the fact that he'd been so captivated by the sexy and solo wedding guest, it had never occurred to him to consider the potential risks of going home with someone he'd only just met—and it should have.

"Did you find anything interesting?" Trevor asked his brother now.

Devin shook his head. "She has almost no social media presence. In fact, she hasn't posted anything to her Facebook page since she adopted a cat a few months back.

"Her sister, on the other hand, is constantly tweeting or Instagramming, sharing pictures of various events that she's planned, hashtag Gilmore Galas."

Trevor hadn't known that Haylee had a cat—or a sister. Because they hadn't wasted a lot of time on conversation. In fact, once they'd gone back to her room at the Stagecoach Inn, they'd done very little talking. They'd been so hot for one another that they'd barely made it inside the door before they were tearing at one another's clothes.

His heart had almost stopped when he'd peeled that sexy dress off her and discovered the even sexier lace she'd been wearing beneath it. The Brazilian panties and plunge bra (yes, he'd spent enough time on the Victoria's Secret website when he was a curious teenager to recognize the styles) were constructed of an almost-sheer fabric with a few strategically placed floral lace appliques. Intrigued, aroused, he'd tumbled with her onto the mattress, then focused his attention on a closer perusal of her undergarments. He'd suckled her breasts through the barely there fabric, moving from one to the other, drawing her turgid nipples into his mouth, gently laving and pulling, making her writhe and moan.

As his mouth skimmed lower, his hands lifted to her breasts, his thumbs continuing to stroke and tease. When his tongue traced the low-cut front of her panty, her hips had lifted off the mattress, wordlessly encouraging him to continue his exploration. So he'd nudged her thighs farther apart and settled between them, eager to taste—

"What happened then?" Devin asked again, interrupting his erotic recollection.

What happened was that Trevor had spent the next several hours with an amazing and passionate woman who'd later disappeared from his life as suddenly and unexpectedly as she'd come into it.

But he didn't want to talk about Haylee—or even

think about her abrupt vanishing act—anymore. Instead he said, "What happened, according to the rumors I heard, is that you finally got up the courage to ask Grace to dance that night."

"Actually, she asked me," Devin admitted.

"And you said yes?" Trevor prompted.

"Yeah." The hint of a smile curved his brother's lips. "I did."

"Were her feet black-and-blue by the time the song was over?"

"If they were, she didn't complain," Devin said, just a little defensively. "And after we danced, we talked for a long time—"

"Probably because her feet couldn't handle any more dancing," Trevor interjected.

"And then," Devin continued, pointedly ignoring the interruption. "I kissed her...or maybe she kissed me. Either way—" his brother shrugged, his lips curving again "—we kissed."

"So maybe she's the reason you suggested a trip to New York," Trevor mused.

Now Devin shook his head. "I told you—and Grace—that I'm not looking for a long-distance relationship."

"Is the distance really the problem? Or is it that you've been alone with your computer for so long that you don't know how to interact with a female?"

He knew he shouldn't tease his brother about his lack of a social life. In fact, he should be grateful that Devin was a homebody because it meant that Trevor had somewhere to go when he didn't feel like hanging out at the bar. And the truth was, he'd been spending a lot more time at Devin's than Diggers' in recent years.

"Oakland isn't a quarter as far as New York," Devin pointed out now. "So what's your excuse?"

"I don't do relationships. Period," Trevor reminded him. But he did have a reputation to uphold, which was why he hung out at his brother's house rather than alone at home.

"You can't let one bad experience—"

"When you've had a fiancée throw a three-carat diamond back in your face and blame you for everything that's ever gone wrong in her life, you can talk to me about bad experiences," he said, abruptly cutting off what was sure to be another one of his brother's pep talks.

"Point taken," Devin said, sounding chagrined.

Trevor didn't feel guilty about using his broken engagement as a tool to shut down the conversation. Though his relationship with Alannis had ended more than four years earlier, only a few weeks after his fiancée had suffered a miscarriage, most of his friends and family continued to tiptoe around the subject. None of them knew the whole truth about what had happened, because Trevor would rather they believed he was still nursing a broken heart than acknowledge that he'd been played for a fool by his supposedly devoted fiancée.

He pushed himself up off the sofa now, eager to escape the direction of his thoughts. "I'm going to get another beer," he announced. "Do you want one?"

"Sure," Devin agreed. "Grab the chips and salsa while you're there, too."

"How many hands do you think I have?"

"As many as you have feet capable of making two trips," Devin said, but he rose, too, and followed his brother into the kitchen.

"Have you talked to Haylee since she went back to California?" he asked, reaching into the cupboard for a bowl.

"You're like a starving dog with a juicy bone, aren't you?"

"Have you?" Devin pressed.

Trevor opened the fridge and pulled out two bottles of beer. "No."

"So give her a call."

"Maybe I will," he said, because it seemed the most likely response to get his brother to drop the subject. And because he was unwilling to admit that he didn't have her number.

In any event, that was a minor impediment. He was confident that he'd be able to track her down, if he really wanted to. He just hadn't yet decided if he wanted to.

And maybe he was a little bit disappointed that she hadn't reached out to him, especially considering that she was the one who'd slipped out of the hotel room they'd shared without even saying goodbye.

He should be relieved.

He *was* relieved.

He was also frustrated and angry and spending far too much time thinking about a woman who'd clearly not spared him a single thought since she'd gone back to California.

He should put her out of his mind.

Instead, he took his beer back to the living room,

pulled up the Athletics' schedule on his phone again and bought two tickets to a baseball game.

Finley snagged a still-warm peanut butter cookie from the tray, sighing with pleasure as she bit into it. "I'm probably going to regret asking, but I have to know—what happened?"

Haylee paused in the act of transferring cookies from the baking sheet to the cooling rack to glance at her sister. "What do you mean?"

"I mean that you're stress baking."

"I'm not," she denied, returning her attention to her task.

"You always start measuring and mixing when you're upset or concerned about something," Finley pointed out. "Because it focuses your attention on something other than whatever is upsetting or concerning you.

"Not that I'm complaining," she assured her sister. "Why would I when I reap the delicious benefits? But since this is the third batch of cookies this week, I can't deny that I'm starting to worry."

"There's no reason for you to worry," Haylee told her.

Finley snagged another cookie. "I beg to differ. And now that I think about it…the baking started three weeks ago, after you got back from Haven."

"That's ridiculous," she said.

"And you've been sketchy with details about your weekend away," Finley continued in support of her argument.

"Sketchy with details?" Haylee echoed disbelievingly. "I took hundreds of pictures at the wedding and showed them all to you."

"And blushed like a schoolgirl when I asked you to point out all the sexy cowboys that you danced with."

"You know I'm more comfortable on the sidelines than the middle of a dance floor."

"Uh-huh," her sister agreed, popping the last bite of cookie into her mouth. "A fact that skirts around rather than answers the question."

"Since you brought up the subject of dancing," Haylee said, in a not-at-all subtle effort to shift the topic of conversation. "How was your date with Thomas last night?"

Finley sighed. "It was a disaster."

"That bad?" she asked, sincerely disappointed for her sibling. She knew how much Finley had been looking forward to the night out and how excited she'd been about spending more time with the guy she'd met a few weeks earlier.

Her sister nodded. "He actually flossed on the dance floor."

"Maybe he had something stuck in his teeth?" Haylee suggested hesitantly.

Finley chuckled. "I mean, he did the floss dance."

"I'm unfamiliar with that one," she admitted.

"You know the chicken dance?"

She nodded.

"Well the floss makes the chicken dance look like a well-choreographed ballet."

"I can't imagine," she admitted with a smile.

"But damn, he's a good kisser," Finley said, sounding sincerely regretful. "In fact, he's so good that when he was kissing me, I almost forgot about what an awful dancer he is."

"Are you going to see him again?"

"I haven't decided, though we're definitely *not* going out dancing again."

"But that's your favorite date night activity," Haylee noted.

"Second favorite," her sister said, with a grin. "And a guy who kisses so expertly and thoroughly most likely has serious skills in the bedroom."

Haylee had to admit that her own, albeit very limited, experience supported her sister's supposition.

Because Trevor Blake had been an amazing kisser.

And an amazing lover.

His mouth had been soft but firm as it moved over hers, coaxing more than demanding. His kiss had been so much more than that simple word entailed; it had been an unexpectedly sweet and irresistible seduction. And from the first brush of his lips against hers, she'd been under his spell. Not just willing but eager. Desperately yearning.

But yearning for what?

She hadn't been entirely sure—she'd only known that she wanted to take everything he offered.

More.

When his tongue had touched the seam of her lips, they'd parted instinctively. Desire had flooded her system, racing through her veins like a drug, making her heart pound and her knees weak. And when he'd drawn her closer, she'd melted against him, holding on to him as the world spun around her.

She'd wanted to blame the champagne, but the truth was, she'd had only one glass, so she knew it wasn't the bubbly alcohol that was responsible for her reaction but the man himself. And—

"And there you go again," Finley said, sounding exasperated.

Haylee snapped back to the present. "What?"

"What is going on with you?" her sister demanded.

"Nothing." She shook her head. "I'm sorry."

"I believe you're sorry. I don't believe it's nothing. So why won't you tell me what it is?" Finley asked, sounding hurt. "I thought we could talk to one another about anything."

"We can," Haylee assured her. "I'm just not sure it's worth talking about."

"Let me be the judge of that."

"Okay," she finally agreed, almost relieved to be able to share at least some of the details with her sister. "If I've been a little distracted since I got back, it's because… I met someone at the wedding."

"Someone tall, dark and handsome?" her sister asked, immediately intrigued and eager for details.

"Unbelievably handsome," she said, almost sighing as a mental picture of Trevor Blake filled her mind. "But I'd describe his hair as more sandy than dark, and his eyes are the color of semisweet chocolate."

"That's pretty specific," Finley noted, sounding amused. "And also, I happen to know, your favorite kind of chocolate."

Haylee couldn't deny it.

"Does this unbelievably handsome guy with chocolate-colored eyes happen to have a name?" her sister asked.

She nodded. "Trevor Blake."

Finley grinned. "Go big or go home, huh?"

"What?"

"Of all the guys to get you hot and bothered, it had to be a Blake."

"The feud is over," she reminded her sister. "And, in any event, it's not likely I'll ever see him again."

"Why would you say that?" Finley challenged. "Haven isn't so far. And you'll be back there again in August for Grandma and Grandpa's sixtieth anniversary."

"I'm sure he'll have forgotten about me long before then," Haylee said, already resigned to the fact.

But she knew that she wouldn't ever forget him and the one amazing night they'd spent together.

What am I doing?

The question nagged at the back of Trevor's mind throughout the seven-hour drive from Haven to Oakland.

Because he knew that the tickets to the baseball game were more a prop than a reason, that the true impetus for this trip was to see Haylee Gilmore.

The world was full of beautiful and interesting women, and he wasn't in the habit of chasing after any of them. But he wasn't chasing the unforgettable brunette from his cousin's wedding so much as he was chasing answers.

Dammit, he was *entitled* to answers.

And he was determined to get them.

But first he had to find her.

There were over a thousand Gilmores in Oakland, and he knew almost nothing about the woman he was looking for aside from her name.

Well, nothing that would help him track her down.

But he knew the scent of her hair, had combed his fingers through the long, silky strands. He knew the taste of her lips, had been intoxicated by her sweet, seductive flavor. He knew the softness of her skin, the sexy sounds she made low in her throat, and he knew how her body felt, wrapped around his.

But the one detail that was indelibly imprinted on his memory, the real reason he'd made this trip to California in search of answers, was that smart, sexy, irresistible Haylee Gilmore had neglected to share an important piece of information when she'd invited him back to her hotel room that night.

She'd failed to tell him that she was a virgin.

Chapter Four

Haylee's plan for Saturday afternoon was to do absolutely nothing. Unfortunately that plan was thwarted by her sister almost as soon as Haylee settled on the sofa with Simon.

She didn't need to pick up the phone to know it was Finley who was calling, because she'd assigned specific ringtones to her various family members and closest friends. She also knew that her sister was at an event, so she wasn't calling just to chat.

"What did you forget?" Haylee asked, as soon as she'd connected the call.

Finley had left early that morning to supervise the arrangement of flowers at the church for an afternoon wedding and ensure the bride's room was ready for her arrival. Though her sister was ruthlessly organized and kept a well-stocked emergency kit of essentials in the trunk of her car, this wouldn't be the first time she'd called Haylee to request something that wasn't in her emergency kit: Big Apple Red nail polish, a bottle of non-aerosol hairspray or Peach Bellini–flavored gourmet jelly beans to soothe an anxious bride.

Of course, Finley had two assistants who worked for her now, so it was rare that she tapped Haylee to run errands these days.

"A plus-one for the bride's brother," Finley said.

"You want me to find a date for some random stranger?"

"No, I want you to *be* his date," her sister clarified.

"I'm going to have to say 'no' to that," Haylee said.

"*Pleeease*," Finley said, drawing out the word. "I'm desperate."

"It sounds to me like the bride's brother is desperate. And why is it your responsibility to find him a date, anyway?" she wondered. "Can't he enjoy his sister's wedding without a girl hanging off his arm?"

"That was the plan," her sister told her. "Until—at the rehearsal dinner last night—he found out that his former fiancée is going to be at the wedding with the groom's brother."

She rolled her eyes at the ceiling. "It sounds like the plotline of a poorly scripted soap opera."

"I know," Finley admitted. "But I promised the bride and groom that I would go above and beyond to make this day perfect for them."

"You make the same promise to everyone who hires you to plan an event," Haylee pointed out. "But you've never tried to pimp me out before."

"And because I make that promise," her sister continued, ignoring the latter part of Haylee's remark, "I'm booked solid for the next fifteen months."

"Yet you never considered the possibility that I might have plans for tonight."

"I considered it," Finley said. "But cuddling with Simon and bingeing on Netflix doesn't count."

"Simon and I beg to differ," she said, stroking a hand down the calico's back.

"Christopher's a really nice guy," her sister said, her tone cajoling. "And not hard to look at, either."

"I'm sure he is, but I don't know him—or anyone else who's going to be at this wedding," Haylee argued. "Plus, I have nothing to wear."

"The dress you bought for Caleb and Brielle's wedding would be perfect."

"It's at the cleaners."

"It was," Finley acknowledged. "I picked it up along with my dry cleaning yesterday. It's now hanging in the front closet."

Haylee sighed. "It's going to take me at least an hour and a half to shave my legs and do my hair and makeup."

"You've got sixty minutes."

Which was really all the time she needed, but she knew that if she'd told her sister she wanted an hour, Finley would have whittled that time down to forty-five minutes.

"Where am I going?" she asked now. "And how long is it going to take me to get there?"

"The reception is in the grand ballroom of the Courtland Hotel. He'll pick you up in an hour."

"Wouldn't it be easier if I met him there?"

"It might be easier, but if you don't show up with him, how will anyone know that you're together? Plus, if he's picking you up, I know you won't accidentally-on-purpose get lost on the way."

Haylee sighed. "Then say goodbye now so I can start getting ready."

"Goodbye," Finley dutifully echoed. "See you soon."

Fifty-five minutes later, Haylee tucked her phone, keys, ID and credit card into her purse and stepped outside to wait for Christopher.

She hadn't thought to ask what kind of car the bride's brother would be driving and was just about to text that question to her sister when a glossy black SUV slowed at the curb. Assuming it was her ride, she automatically started toward the end of the driveway.

Then the driver's side door opened and a familiar—albeit unexpected—figure emerged.

Her heart skipped a beat, then kicked hard against her ribs. "Trevor?"

The door slammed shut and he took a few steps closer, his gaze skimming over her, from the deliberately loose knot of hair to the pink dress and the strappy sandals on her feet. A smile curved his lips. "Déjà vu."

"What are you doing here?" she asked, determinedly ignoring the fluttery sensation in her belly.

"Looking for you," he said.

Her heart skipped another two beats, and all her girl parts sighed with longing.

"But I'm getting the feeling that I may have come at a bad time," he continued.

"Yeah," she admitted, deeply and sincerely regretful. "I'm on my way out…a favor for my sister."

She didn't want to call it a date, because it really wasn't. And though she hadn't seen or even spoken to Trevor since the night they'd spent together in her hotel room, she wasn't comfortable admitting that her plans included another guy.

"How about tomorrow then?" he asked.

"Tomorrow?" she echoed, her mind blank.

"Do you have any plans tomorrow? Because I've got an extra ticket to the baseball game, if you want to join me."

"You came all this way for a baseball game?"

"My brother and I usually make the trip a couple times a year, but he had to go out of town for a conference this weekend, so I'm on my own."

Obviously he enjoyed driving more than she did, as she'd chosen to fly to Haven for the wedding rather than spend almost seven hours behind the wheel of a car with no one for company.

"So…what do you say to catching a ball game tomorrow? The A's are playing the Rangers," he said, as if that additional bit of information might influence her response. "I'll even buy you a hot dog."

She managed a smile. "Now that's a tempting offer."

"Is that a *yes*?" he prompted hopefully.

Of course she wanted to say *yes*. She was thrilled to see him again, eager to believe that he'd sought her out because the night they'd spent together had meant as much to him as it had to her. Except that she wasn't the type of girl that a guy went out of his way to spend time with—and five hundred miles was definitely out of his way.

"Why are you really here, Trevor?"

He smiled again. "I'm a diehard A's fan." Then his expression turned serious. "But I also think there are some things that we need to talk about."

She swallowed uneasily. "You do?"

He pinned her with his gaze. "Don't you?"

Before she could respond, her phone buzzed inside her purse. "I need to check that."

Not surprisingly, it was a text message from her sister.

Christopher will be there in 2 min. Are you ready?

She tapped a quick reply.

Ready and waiting.

"Obviously our conversation will have to wait," Trevor noted.

"I'm sorry."

"No need to apologize. I should have realized that you'd have plans on a Saturday night."

She didn't tell him that it was a rare event, instead asking, "What time's the game tomorrow?"

"One-oh-five," he said. "How about if I swing by to pick you up around noon?"

"Actually, I've got to check in at a worksite not too far from the coliseum in the morning, so it probably makes more sense for me to meet you there."

He pulled his phone out of his back pocket. "I'll send

you the e-ticket so that we can meet at our seats rather than trying to connect outside."

"Sounds good," she said.

He swiped the screen, then looked at her. "I'm going to need your number."

"Oh, right." She felt her cheeks flush as she rattled off the digits.

A few seconds later, her phone pinged to indicate receipt of his message with the ticket attached. At the same time, a silver-colored sports car pulled up at the curb. "That's my ride."

Trevor took a step back, a slightly puzzled expression on his face. "I'll see you tomorrow then?"

She nodded, already looking forward to it.

The next morning, Trevor had breakfast at his hotel near the Oakland Alameda County Coliseum, then checked out of his room and headed over to the ballpark. He still had a couple hours to kill before the game's official start time, and he didn't like to admit that he'd probably spend most of that time thinking about Haylee.

When he'd embarked on this road trip, he'd been looking forward to not just the baseball game but reconnecting with the woman who'd preoccupied his thoughts since the night they'd spent together. Yes, he wanted answers from her. But he also just wanted to see her and maybe, if the attraction between them was as strong as he remembered, get naked with her again and take his time teaching her to appreciate all the things he wouldn't have rushed through the first time if he'd known it was her first time.

It was obviously a testament to his own inflated

sense of self that he'd never considered that she might already have other plans—and not want to abandon them to be with him. He'd definitely never considered that those plans might be a date with another guy. Because notwithstanding what she'd said about a favor for her sister, it hadn't been her sister driving the silver sports car that picked her up—it had been a man.

Trevor might have thought it was an Uber or Lyft, except that drivers for hire didn't usually drive luxury vehicles. Plus this one had been wearing a suit, as he'd observed when the driver got out of the car to open the passenger-side door for Haylee.

She didn't glance in Trevor's direction as she lowered herself into the vehicle, so she didn't see him standing on the sidewalk with what was undoubtedly a *WTF* expression on his face and even more questions swirling in his mind.

The biggest one right now was: Would she use the ticket he gave her—or would the seat beside his remain empty throughout the game?

He scowled at the thought as his own ticket was scanned.

He could tell himself that he'd sought Haylee out not just for answers but because he felt guilty about taking her innocence. But the truth was, he'd been drawn to her from the start. From the first moment he'd set eyes on her at Brielle and Caleb's wedding, he'd been intrigued. By the time they'd danced together under the stars, in a field beside a field of cows, he'd been smitten.

And then he'd been dumped.

At least, it sure as hell felt that way.

So maybe his heart wasn't bruised so much as his pride was stung.

Except that even his brief interaction with Haylee the day before suggested there was more going on than a dent to his ego. There was definitely something between them—a spark that hadn't been extinguished despite the time and distance that had passed since they parted ways. So he really hoped she showed up today, because he knew that he wouldn't be going back to Nevada without seeing her again, and he was afraid he'd be venturing close to stalker territory if he showed up at her door a second time.

He shifted his attention to the field as the home team took their positions for warm-up. He still remembered his first major league game—an opening day contest at this very stadium when he was just ten years old. It had been a father-son trip, just Elijah Blake and Trevor, and one of his happiest early memories.

Devin had protested that he was a son, too, but their dad had remained firm. "Your turn will come," he'd promised his second-born. And it had, two years later, when Devin had reached the milestone of double digits.

After that, opening day had become an annual ritual for the three of them, and this park held a lot of wonderful memories: the sound of a ball coming off the sweet spot of a bat; a leaping over-the-wall catch that robbed a visiting hitter of a home run; a quick throw to pick off a base runner; an unexpected walk-off home run from the bottom of the lineup.

There were a lot of reasons that baseball was America's favorite pastime, and when Trevor and Devin were old enough to finance their own travels, the brothers started making additional trips to California to savor the glory of the game. They occasionally visited other parks, too, but the Athletics were their team—for better or for worse.

Thinking about his brother now, he pulled out his phone to check in with Devin.

How are things in Montreal?

Très occupé.

Trevor smiled at the response.

I just wanted you to know that while you're stuck in a conference room, I'm at the A's game and the sun is shining.

Tabarnak!

Trevor had no idea what that was supposed to mean, but the exclamation mark suggested that it was a curse of some kind.

Devin switched back to English then to ask:

Who's there with you? ;)

A stadium full of people I've never met before.

That got him an eye roll emoji, followed by:

Did you buy one ticket or two?

Trevor wasn't sure he wanted to answer that question—especially as the seat beside him was currently still unoccupied. Instead, he replied:

They're announcing the national anthem singer. I'll catch up with you later.

Enjoy the game.

He glanced at the time displayed on the top of his screen before he tucked his phone away and rose to his feet. The exchange with his brother had managed to divert his attention for a whole three minutes, which meant that it was now three minutes closer to the throwing out of the ceremonial first pitch—and there was still no sign of Haylee .

Chapter Five

She was late.

Haylee glanced at the electronic ticket on the screen of her phone again as she navigated through the thinning crowd in search of the entrance to Section 120. It had to be close to game time, as groups of spectators were moving away from the concession stands, carrying trays of food and drinks, toward their seats in the stadium.

The scents of grilled meat and greasy fries made her stomach growl, but she didn't stop. Not only because she worried that she was already late, but because her stomach—though empty—was also jittery about the prospect of seeing Trevor again.

Anticipation, yes, but a little bit of trepidation, too, as the echo of his words "we need to talk" reverberated inside her head. She was pretty sure she knew what the "some things" he wanted to talk about were—or at least *one* of the things. And it wasn't a topic that she was particularly eager to discuss.

She'd slipped out of her room at the Stagecoach Inn in the early hours of the morning without waking him because she was a coward, because she didn't want to answer the questions she knew he would ask. And though it still wasn't a conversation she was eager to have, she couldn't resist the opportunity to spend more time with him.

She showed her ticket to an usher, to ensure she was headed in the right direction. He nodded and smiled. "Enjoy the game."

"Thanks."

The crowd was restless, eager for the game to start—which meant that she wasn't actually late. Not yet.

She looked around, scanning the crowd. There were groups of men, couples, families, an elderly couple down by the third base line, decked out from head to toe in Athletics' gear. She'd never really understood the desire to display one's team allegiance, but she'd borrowed a T-shirt and baseball cap from her sister's closet—to blend in but also because she hadn't known what else to wear to a baseball game.

She could have asked Finley's advice, but then she'd have to admit that she had a date—if an invitation to a baseball game could be considered a date.

Which it probably wasn't.

Hopefully wasn't.

Because in addition to not knowing what to wear, she'd been so focused on getting to the job site that she hadn't thought to put on makeup before she'd left home earlier that morning. It wasn't until she was on her way to the coliseum that she wished she'd taken the time to brush some mascara onto her lashes and swipe some gloss on her lips.

Of course, most women carried those essentials in their purses so that they could freshen up their look at any point during the day, but Haylee wasn't most women. Her morning beauty routine consisted of slapping on some moisturizer with sunscreen, because she never knew when she might be working outside in the elements, and untinted lip balm.

Well, today Trevor Blake was going to meet the real Haylee Gilmore, and if he didn't like what he saw, he was going to be on his way back to Haven soon enough anyway.

She counted her way to Row 25, then looked for Seat 10. She spotted Trevor first, and the empty spot beside him.

"Excuse me," she said, sidling past the already seated spectators.

With every shuffling step, her heart began to beat just a little bit faster, until she finally reached the vacant seat beside him just as the crowd rose for the singing of the national anthem.

"Sorry I'm late," she said, after the anthem had concluded and they were settled into their seats.

"You weren't actually late," he pointed out.

"Then I'll apologize for cutting it close," she amended.

"No need," he said. "I'm just glad you made it. And

curious what you do for an electrical company that required you to work on a Sunday morning."

"We had to install a new breaker panel at a local law office, and they wanted it done before Monday."

"So you're an electrician," he realized.

She nodded.

"Why didn't you just say so in the first place?" he wondered.

"Because Finley told me that some guys are intimidated by women who work in what are traditionally viewed as male occupations," she admitted.

"Who's Finley? And why are you taking advice from her?"

"My sister," she said. "And because she's my sister."

"Even so, why would you want to be with a guy who felt threatened by your job?"

"I wouldn't," she assured him. "But it's hard to argue with a sister who has a lot more dating experience than I do."

"Well, speaking as a guy with a fair amount of dating experience, I have to confess a weakness for women who aren't just beautiful but interesting."

"Then you'd like my sister," Haylee noted.

Of course, all the guys she'd ever liked had liked Finley better. And she didn't doubt that if Finley had attended the wedding in Haven, Trevor wouldn't have looked at Haylee twice.

He shook his head, a slight smile curving his lips. "I like you, Haylee."

Her heart thumped against her ribs and heat rushed through her veins. "You do?"

"Yes, I do," he confirmed. "Why else would I give you my extra ticket?"

"Because you don't know anyone else in Oakland."

Trevor couldn't help but chuckle at that.

"Because I wanted to see you," he clarified.

"And I didn't even put on any makeup today."

The blurted confession was immediately followed by a rush of color to her cheeks.

"Which only proves you don't need it. And as much as I like you in a dress and heels, this is a good look for you, too," he said, gesturing to the enormous gold-colored *A* emblazoned on the front of her dark green T-shirt and matching ball cap.

"I borrowed the T-shirt and hat from Finley's closet," she confided.

"Your sister's a fan?"

"She dated one of the players—Mark Nickel—a few years back. They broke up when he was traded to Baltimore."

"She couldn't bring herself to cheer for the Orioles?" he guessed.

"She didn't want a long-distance relationship."

"California to Maryland is quite a distance," he acknowledged, even as he wondered if Haylee was trying to make a point about the fact that they lived in different states.

Not that he was looking for a relationship, but he wouldn't view five hundred miles as an insurmountable barrier, and he didn't like to think that she'd already closed herself off to the possibility of something more between them. After all, most women thought he was quite a catch.

But that might be because he was a big fish in a small pond in Haven and Haylee was accustomed to more plentiful waters in Oakland. Except that she obviously hadn't done much fishing in those waters, as he'd discovered when he shared her bed.

Which was, of course, what he'd wanted to talk to her about. But listening to the buzz of the crowd around them, he realized that this wasn't the best time or place to get into a conversation about why she hadn't told him about her inexperience and then disappeared without even a goodbye the morning after.

He was still justifiably annoyed with her about that, but right now he was having trouble remembering his annoyance. Because he could smell just a hint of coconut in her shampoo, and he recalled that same scent lingering on the pillow where she'd lain her head. And he could see the sweet curve of her breasts beneath her T-shirt and was certain the scripted *A* had never looked so good. The hem of the shirt was tucked into slim-fitting jeans, and on her feet, she wore dark brown work boots—steel-toed, he'd bet, now that he knew what her job entailed. And while he appreciated a woman in sexy heels as much as the next guy, thinking about the contrast of Haylee's delicate feet with pink-painted toenails inside those heavy boots was a surprising turn-on.

She leaned forward in her seat as the batter's swing connected with the ball, sending it sailing through the air, deep into center field. But not quite deep enough, as the fielder's glove swallowed it on the warning track.

"Whew." She settled back again. "That was a little too close for comfort."

"Apparently the manager thought so, too," he noted,

as the man jogged out to the mound to talk to his pitcher, and only then realizing that he'd been paying more attention to the woman seated beside him than the action on the field.

"He can't call for a pitching change already," she protested. "That would put too much pressure on the bullpen."

"So much for thinking that I might impress you with my detailed knowledge of the game," he noted dryly.

"Sorry," she immediately apologized. "I'm not very good at sitting quiet and looking pretty."

"That isn't something you should ever apologize for," he assured her. "Although I'd have to disagree with the latter part of your claim."

"But now you've impressed me with your use of the word 'latter.' Most of the guys I work with only know it as a set of horizontal bars used for climbing up or down."

"I'll take points wherever I can get them," he said.

"You'd get bonus points for feeding me," Haylee told him.

"Are you hungry?"

"Starving," she admitted.

"You want a hot dog?"

"I'd love a hot dog."

"I'll head to the concession stand as soon as the top of the inning is over," he promised. "What do you like on your dog?"

"Ketchup and mustard. Please."

"And to drink?"

"A Coke would be great, thanks."

"I'll be right back," he promised.

Of course, he missed the better part of two innings waiting in line for their food, and the A's had taken a two-run lead by the time he returned, carrying a tray with two dogs, two Cokes, a heaping box of fries, a bag of roasted-in-the-shell peanuts and a package of licorice.

He put one of the cups in her cupholder, then handed her a foil-wrapped dog. "Thanks."

She eagerly unwrapped it, but paused when he set the bag of peanuts and the licorice in her lap. "What are those for?"

"Extra bonus points?" he suggested.

She chuckled as she lifted the hot dog to her mouth. When she finished chewing, she took a long swallow of soda. Watching her mouth close over the straw made him want to imagine those same lips closing around

No. Not the time or place to indulge in prurient fantasies, he chastised himself, and turned his attention to his own lunch and the ball game.

It had been a couple of years since Haylee had last been at the coliseum for a baseball game. And while she occasionally caught the action on TV, the live experience was so much better. Sitting beside Trevor while watching the game was even better still.

But by the seventh inning stretch, the A's were holding a three-run edge over the Rangers, the food wrappers and beverage containers were empty and Haylee's stomach was feeling a little unsettled. It was her own fault, she knew, for racing out of the house without breakfast and then stuffing her face with everything Trevor had brought back from the concession stand.

Not that she'd eaten it all, but she'd consumed at least her fair share.

Still, she stood when everyone else did, eager to stretch her legs and restore some circulation to her bottom. But she must have moved too quickly, because the earth seemed to shift beneath her feet, forcing her to grab hold of the seatback in front of her for balance. Or she'd spent too much time in the sun. Or maybe too much time in close proximity to a hunky weekend cowboy who actually seemed to be interested in *her*.

Several times throughout the game, she'd glanced over to find his gaze on her rather than the action playing out on the field. But thankfully, he hadn't noticed her tilting off balance, and a few minutes later, they were seated again.

As the crowd roared in appreciation of the home team executing a textbook 4-6-3 play that put them within one out of the win, she glanced over at Trevor with a happy smile and found his attention focused on her.

"Why are you looking at me rather than the baseball game that you traveled five hundred miles to see?" she asked.

"Because you're a lot prettier than anyone on the field."

Unaccustomed to such compliments, she felt her cheeks flush. "You obviously missed the double play that just happened, because it was truly a thing of beauty."

"You obviously haven't considered that maybe the game was just an excuse to see you," he suggested.

She couldn't help but laugh at that.

"You don't think it's true?" he challenged.

"A few years back, I dated a guy who grumbled about having to drive from Chabot Park to Glenview to spend time with me," she told him. "So forgive me for not believing that you'd come all the way from Haven, Nevada, for the pleasure of my company."

"I have no idea how far Chabot Park is from Glenview—"

"About ten miles," she interjected.

"—but I'm sure the guy was an idiot," he continued.

"Or maybe he just wasn't that into me," she allowed, as the Rangers' potential final batter set up at the plate. "Although, in all fairness, I wasn't that into him, either."

"How long were you together?"

The first pitch was off the plate on the inside for a ball.

"We went out four or five times over the space of about three months."

"Four or five?" he asked, sounding amused. "You don't remember?"

The second pitch was high. Ball two.

"We ran into one another by chance one night when we were both waiting for a table at a new restaurant. We were both with friends and decided to eat together. I'm not sure that actually counts as a date."

"Did he drive you home after dinner?"

"No."

Trevor shifted his attention to the plate as the umpire finally called "stee-rike" on the third pitch. "Did he kiss you goodbye?"

"On the cheek."

He shook his head then. "Definitely not a date."

"Those are the criteria?" she asked. "Taking a girl home and kissing her goodbye?"

"At the very least."

After watching the first three pitches go by, the batter finally took a swing at the ball—and missed. Strike two.

"Then I've been on even fewer dates than I realized," she mused.

And when the batter swung again at an outside pitch for the third strike and final out, she was a little disappointed that this one—though not technically a date—was over.

"It's hard to complain when the home team wins," she remarked, as they shuffled toward the exit with the rest of the departing spectators. "But it sucked for Ramirez that he didn't get to bat in the ninth and have a chance to hit for the cycle."

"Most team players would say it's the win that matters."

"And they'd be lying," Haylee said, making him laugh.

"Seriously," she continued. "Giants fans who remember August 7, 2007, know it as the date that Barry Bonds hit home run number 756 to break Hank Aaron's record, but I bet most of them couldn't tell you the final score of that game—or even who won."

"Fair point," he acknowledged, guiding her toward the northside exits as the crowd began to disperse.

"The BART station is that way," she said, pointing.

"But the lot I'm parked in is this way," he said, nudging her forward.

"Then I guess we should say goodbye here."

"We'll say goodbye after I've taken you home," he said.

"There's no reason for you to go out of your way," she protested. "And I'm sure you're anxious to be getting back to your hotel."

"Actually, I've got a ten o'clock meeting tomorrow morning, so I'm heading back to Haven tonight."

"Then I definitely don't want to delay your departure."

"My father taught me to always see a girl safely to her door," he said.

"One of the criteria for a date," she noted, butterflies winging around inside her tummy at the thought that he might want to kiss her goodbye.

"And if you invited me to come inside for a cup of coffee—to help keep me awake for the long drive home—I could kiss you goodbye without any concerns about your neighbors watching."

"I could make you a cup of coffee," she agreed, as he walked her around to the passenger side of his vehicle. He clicked a button on the key fob to unlock the door, then reached for the handle, as if to open it for her.

"Is something wrong?" she asked when he paused.

"I'm definitely going to want a cup of coffee when we get to your place," he said, lifting a hand to tip the brim of her ball cap up as he lowered his head. "But I don't want to wait that long to kiss you."

Chapter Six

And just like the first time Trevor had kissed her, Haylee responded with a passion that roused his own. He wrapped his arms around her, to draw her closer, but she was already there, the soft curves of her body melting against him. He touched the tip of his tongue to the seam of her lips, and they parted willingly for him to deepen the kiss.

She lifted her arms and twined her hands behind his head, holding on to him as she kissed him back.

For the past several weeks, he'd been beating himself up over the fact that he'd taken her to bed—and taken her virginity—without ever guessing the extent of her inexperience.

No matter how often he told himself that he couldn't have known what she didn't tell him, he couldn't shake the feeling that he should have picked up on signs or signals. He had enough experience with women to recognize inexperience, but Haylee's passionate responses to every kiss and touch had blinded him to all else.

Maybe she'd seemed a little overeager, but he'd chalked that up to the champagne, guessing that she was just a little bit tipsy. But not too tipsy—he would never have accepted the invitation to go back to her hotel if he'd suspected that she was drunk.

And he definitely wouldn't have accepted her invitation if he'd suspected that she was a virgin.

In retrospect, the pieces all fit together to form a clear picture. But in the moment, when she'd been panting his name, her nails raking down his back, her body arching to meet his, he hadn't been thinking clearly. He'd barely been able to think at all.

He'd wanted her with a desperation he hadn't felt since he was a seventeen-year-old virgin eager to change that status. And when she'd lifted her hips off the mattress, he hadn't hesitated to accept the wordless invitation. He'd buried himself in her, ramming through the barrier of her virginity before his brain had a chance to register the unexpected resistance.

And by then, it was too late.

He'd heard her gasp of shock—or was it pain?—and immediately tried to withdraw. But she'd thwarted his best efforts, wrapping her arms and legs around him, drawing him even deeper inside her. And the glorious feeling of being deep inside her completely wiped from his mind any thought of pulling away.

But afterward, he didn't know what to say to her.

He'd been in shock. Stunned. Furious. Confused.

And so, when he'd returned to the bedroom after disposing of the condom marked with the evidence of her lost innocence and found her pretending to be asleep, he went along with the pretense, confident that he would get the answers he deserved in the morning.

Three weeks later, he still didn't have any answers. But he had Haylee in his arms, and right now, nothing else seemed to matter.

"Get a room." The suggestion was made in a derisive tone and from close proximity. "Or at least get out of my way."

Haylee had already pulled out of Trevor's arms, flattening herself against the passenger door of his SUV so the rude stranger could enter the adjacent vehicle.

Trevor resisted the urge to flip the guy off, acknowledging that he should be grateful for the interruption because he wasn't sure how far he would have gone in the middle of the afternoon in a busy parking lot—especially when Haylee had given no indication of wanting to stop him.

"I'll apologize for the poor choice of venue but not for the kiss," Trevor told her. "I've been wanting to do that all day."

Haylee blinked, surprised by the admission. "You have?"

"Actually, I've been thinking about it since I saw you yesterday," he confided, and lightly brushed his mouth over hers again. "Your lips are as soft and sweet as I remembered."

"And your kiss is as bone-melting as I remembered," she said, her head spinning and her knees weak.

He grinned. "I like that you say exactly what's on your mind."

"You do?" she asked dubiously.

"It's a refreshing change," he assured her. "A lot of girls like to make a guy guess what they're thinking—and then punish him for guessing wrong."

"I don't play those kinds of games," Haylee said. "Probably because I don't know the rules."

"Maybe not, but you have some serious skills."

"Do you think so?" she asked, pleased by his assessment.

"I also think it's lucky for we mortal men that you don't understand the true extent of your power," he said, and opened the passenger-side door for her.

As Trevor navigated the heavy flow of traffic leaving the coliseum, Haylee wasn't nervous about going back to her apartment with him because she knew they wouldn't be alone. Although Finley had planned all the minute details for a baptism celebration that afternoon, it was a small event and she'd put her assistant Julia in charge of the execution on-site.

She was, however, a little apprehensive about introducing Trevor to Finley, because no man had ever wanted to be with Haylee after meeting her sister. But maybe that was exactly the reality check Haylee needed. Being with Trevor—flirting with him and kissing him—made her want more. And despite her relative inexperience with men, she recognized that he wasn't the type to give more.

In any event, if he shifted his fickle attention to her sister—as members of the male species were apt to do—she should breathe a sigh of relief. Sure, it had been nice to be the sole focus of a guy's attention, at least for a while. But she knew that she was in way over her head and that Finley was much better equipped to deal with someone like Trevor Blake than Haylee would ever be.

"Nice place," he noted, following her down the flag-stone path that led to an old-fashioned carriage house behind a two-story stone-and-brick mansion.

"We like it," she said.

"You live with your sister?"

She nodded as she slid her key into the lock. "And Simon."

Speaking of, as soon as Trevor stepped into the foyer behind her, the silly animal streaked down the hall and disappeared into an open doorway.

"That was Simon," she told him.

"Cat?" he guessed.

Haylee nodded. "He's usually waiting for me at the door when I come home, but he's wary of strangers and will probably hide under my bed until you're gone."

As she headed to the kitchen, she heard the mur-mur of her sister's voice behind the closed door of her home office.

"You'll get to meet my sister when she's off the phone—if she gets off the phone. She has an event planning business, Gilmore Galas," she explained, as she examined the carousel of K-Cups. "Do you want regular or decaf?"

"Regular," he said. "I've got a long drive ahead of me."

"French roast, Colombian dark, breakfast blend or caramel vanilla?"

"Regular," he said again.

She smiled as she selected the French roast and popped it into the machine.

"Cream or sugar?"

"Yes. Please."

She opened the fridge to get out the cream and found a bag of sugar in the pantry. She set both on the table and grabbed a teaspoon from the drawer.

Finley walked into the kitchen then, looked at the condiments and gave a slight shake of her head.

"Haylee doesn't entertain very often," she said, opening the cupboard above the coffee maker and taking out a small ceramic pitcher and matching covered sugar bowl.

"You must be Finley," he said. "And really, this is fine. Don't get out the fancy dishes for me."

"They're not fancy," she denied. "And you are…"

"Trevor Blake."

She shook his proffered hand. "It's nice to meet you."

"Likewise," he said, smiling his thanks to Haylee when she set a mug of coffee in front of him.

"Cookies are always good with coffee," Finley hinted to her sister.

"Do you want a cookie?" Haylee asked Trevor.

"I think I ate more than enough at the ball game."

"So that's where you were," Finley noted. "Of course, the T-shirt and cap you stole from my closet should have been the giveaway."

"Borrowed," Haylee corrected.

Her sister, clearly undeterred by Trevor's insistence that he wasn't hungry, carefully arranged a handful of cookies on a plate.

"Peanut butter cup cookies," she said, setting the plate on the table with a couple of napkins.

"Homemade," he noted, sounding impressed.

"Haylee made them," Finley told him. "She can't boil water without scorching a pot—"

"That happened once," she interjected, rolling her eyes.

"—but her baked goods are the best. You'll think you've gone to sugar heaven."

"Now I have to try one," Trevor said, reaching for a cookie.

"If you believe the heaven part, you're going to be disappointed," Haylee warned.

He bit into the cookie and hummed a low sound of approval. "I'm not disappointed."

Finley winked. "Told you."

Her phone chimed with a text message. "Whoops! I forgot the guest book when I packed up at the reception last night. I'm going to run over to the hotel now to pick it up before it gets misplaced." She grabbed her purse off a hook by the door and tucked her phone in the side pocket. "It was nice meeting you, Trevor."

"You, too," he said.

But she was already gone, leaving Haylee and Trevor alone.

"Maybe running out without saying goodbye is a family trait," he mused.

Haylee paused with her mug halfway to her mouth.

"That is, after all, what you did the morning after we spent the night together."

"Because I had a plane to catch," she said. "And you were asleep."

"Or maybe because you didn't want to talk about what happened the night before?"

"I don't have a lot of experience with mornings after," she said.

"Or any?" he suggested.

"So it just seemed easier to avoid awkward and unnecessary conversation," she continued, ignoring his question as the answer was obvious.

"I'd argue that it was necessary."

"Why? Because you're accustomed to being the one who walks away in the morning?" she guessed.

He frowned at that. "No, because you were a virgin."

"Please don't make a big deal about that," she pleaded.

"Isn't it a big deal?" he asked.

"No," she responded.

He studied her for a long moment as he sipped his coffee. "How old are you, Haylee?"

"What does my age have to do with anything?" she wondered, baffled by the unexpected question.

"How old?" he asked again.

She huffed out a breath. "Twenty-nine."

"So you were a virgin for twenty-nine years, and then suddenly decided to get naked with a guy you'd met only a few hours earlier?"

"Trust me, that status wasn't deliberate. I wasn't saving it for someone special. I wasn't consciously saving it at all," she confided. "I guess I just…never met anyone that I wanted…to be…intimate with."

"So I should be flattered that you chose me?" he challenged.

"You don't have to be flattered. Just don't make a big deal out of it."

"I'm trying not to," he said. "But I can't understand how you got to be a twenty-nine-year-old virgin."

"By not having sex for twenty-nine years," she said, stating the obvious.

"Seriously," he said. "You can't expect me to believe that you didn't have boyfriends."

"I had a couple," she acknowledged. "I just didn't sleep with any of them."

"Not even the guy you were with last night?"

She frowned. "What are you talking about? Who?"

"The guy who picked you up in front of the house."

"That wasn't a date. It was a favor for my sister."

He lifted a brow.

"I told you she's an event planner," she reminded him. "Yesterday the bride was stressing because she found out that her brother's ex-fiancée was going to be at the wedding as the groom's cousin's plus-one, so Finley promised to find a date for the brother so that he wouldn't be alone."

His gaze narrowed. "You just made that up."

"I did not," she assured him.

"Does your sister often require your help at events?"

"Occasionally. But that was the first time I had to wear a dress and heels. Usually I just run errands. Although I did fill in as a server once, when the caterer was short-staffed."

"A woman of many talents," he mused. Then he shifted gears again to ask, "So…are you currently dating anyone?"

"Well, according to your definition, I had a date this afternoon."

"Nice guy?" he asked, obviously fishing for a compliment.

"Nice enough," she agreed.

"Good-looking?"

She reached for a cookie, fighting against a smile. "I'm sure most women would think so."

"What do *you* think?"

"I think he's way out of my league, and I'll probably never see him again after today."

He appeared to mull over that response as she nibbled on the edge of the cookie. Though they were usually her favorite, her stomach was already protesting the fact that she'd eaten more junk food in one afternoon than she usually consumed in a week.

She set down the cookie and picked up her mug, then put it down again without drinking.

"Excuse me," she said, abruptly pushing away from the table.

Trevor instinctively followed her down the hall, where the unmistakable sound of retching could be heard through the closed door of what he hoped was the bathroom.

He waited for the retching to stop, then tapped on the wood portal. "Haylee?"

She groaned. "Please. Go. Away."

He retreated a few steps but hesitated to go any farther until he heard the toilet flush, then the tap run. As he listened to the sound of what he guessed was her toothbrush, he found himself wondering about her sudden bout of nausea.

Maybe it was paranoia. Or maybe it was the fact that he'd been faced with an all-too-similar situation before. But Trevor suddenly found himself wondering...

Was it possible...could she be...pregnant?

He hadn't realized that he'd spoken aloud or that she'd come out of the bathroom until she responded with an immediate and vehement denial: "No! Of course not."

But he noted that her face had gone pale, as if she was only now considering the possibility.

"We used protection," she said, as if that would put the question to rest.

"A condom that you provided." And recalling that detail, deeply buried memories and ugly suspicions rose to the surface of his mind.

"Because even a girl who's never had sex knows the dangers of unprotected sex," she told him. "That's the only reason I've been carrying a condom with me since the night of my high school prom."

"Please tell me that's not the condom we used."

"Of course not," she denied. "That one's probably still in the purse I took to prom."

"Well, that's a relief," he said, following her back to the kitchen.

She seemed puzzled by his response. "Why does it matter where the condom came from?"

"Because a condom left over from high school would have expired a long time ago."

She swallowed as she sank into the chair she'd recently abandoned. "What do you mean—expired?"

He returned to his seat across from her. "I mean that condoms have a shelf life."

He wouldn't have thought it was possible, but her face got even whiter then.

"Why would you tell me something like that *now*?"

"I didn't realize it would be news to you."

"They shouldn't call it protection if it doesn't protect," she grumbled.

"Did we use an expired condom?" he asked her.

"I don't know…maybe." She nibbled on her bottom lip. "Probably."

He was trying really hard not to overreact, but he also wasn't going to pretend he wasn't pissed by this revelation. "I'm guessing that you're not on any other form of birth control?"

"No," she admitted.

"So it's not outside the realm of possibility that you could be pregnant," he noted.

She shook her head. "No," she said again, though not quite as vehemently this time as color filled her pale cheeks. "I got my period a couple of weeks ago."

"Was your flow normal?"

"Ohmygod." She dropped her face into her hands, clearly uncomfortable with the direction of their conversation. "Why are you doing this?"

"Because I need to know if there's any chance that you might be carrying my child."

"I just told you there's not."

"Sometimes the spotting that can occur early in pregnancy is mistaken for a period."

"How would you know something like that?" she challenged.

"I just do," he said, unwilling to get into the details of that particular history with her right now.

"It wasn't spotting," she said, the pink color in her cheeks deepening. "And I really don't want to talk about this anymore."

He nodded. "Okay. But just so we're clear—I'm not going to marry you."

Her eyes went wide and her jaw fell open, but she recovered quickly and replied, "I don't recall asking you to marry me."

"You didn't," he acknowledged coolly. "But I didn't want you holding on to false hope, in case your seduction at the wedding was all part of some elaborate plan to trap me."

"*My* seduction?" she echoed incredulously. "*You're* the one who followed me into the field."

"And *you're* the one who invited me back to your hotel."

"Obviously that night was a mistake," she snapped back at him now.

"I have no regrets about that night," he told her. "But I'm not going to be on the hook for the next eighteen years because of it."

"I didn't have any regrets, either," she said. "Until you started throwing around outrageous accusations."

"I'm sorry," he said. "But you wouldn't be the first woman who thought she could trap me into marriage."

"How many illegitimate Trevor Blakes are there running around in the world?" she wondered aloud.

"Not even one," he promised.

"And I can assure you, I have no interest in changing that number." She pushed away from the table again. "Since your coffee is obviously finished, you should go. You've got a long drive ahead of you."

Chapter Seven

He'd never been dismissed so completely—and angrily— by a woman.

Three days later, Trevor was still trying to figure out how an enjoyable afternoon at the ballpark had gone so spectacularly wrong. But maybe it wasn't such a mystery. Maybe a man accusing a woman of trying to get pregnant to trap him into marriage wasn't the best way to tell her that he'd like to see her again.

Of course, he hadn't acknowledged the truth of that desire even to himself until he was with her. Yes, he'd gone to California because he'd wanted answers. But he'd also wanted to know what it was about Haylee that had so completely captivated him from the start.

Her parting words suggested that she wasn't nearly as enamored of him, and he could hardly fault her for that. Not considering the things he'd said, the accusations he'd leveled.

Desperate for a reprieve from his own thoughts, Trevor picked up a six-pack and a pizza from Jo's and stopped by to see his brother.

"So tell me about the game," Devin said, as he lifted a slice of three-meat pizza from the box.

Trevor twisted the cap off a bottle and swallowed a mouthful of beer before responding. "The A's won."

"I got that much from the sports recap on the news," his brother said. "I was hoping you could supply a few more details."

"Ramirez almost hit for the cycle."

Devin waved a hand dismissively. "Almost doesn't count."

"He got on base with a double in the second and a triple in the fifth and homered in the seventh," Trevor continued anyway, because as long as he was talking about the game, he didn't have to think about the fact that the rest of his weekend had been a complete bust. "All he needed was a single in the ninth, but the A's didn't have to bat."

"That's an impressive almost," his brother acknowledged. "Remember when we saw Mark Nickel hit for the cycle?"

"Yeah, and then they traded Nickel in the off-season."

"Horrible trade." Devin reached into the box for another slice of pizza. "Did Haylee enjoy the game?"

Trevor froze with his beer halfway to his mouth. "What makes you think I saw Haylee?"

"Come on," his brother said. "We both know she's the real reason you went to California."

He scowled at that as he swallowed a mouthful of beer. "I didn't even realize she was the reason until I was halfway to California."

His brother shrugged. "Proof, yet again, that I've always been smarter than you."

"As if there was ever any doubt."

"Well, for what it's worth, I'm happy to see you showing a real interest in someone again."

"She lives in California," he reminded his brother.

"That's not so far," Devin said. "And it's long past time for you to start dating again."

"What are you talking about? I date."

"Picking up a woman in a bar, sleeping with her and never calling her again isn't really a date."

"I haven't done that in a long time," Trevor pointed out in his defense.

"And you haven't had a real relationship since…"

"Since Alannis?" he guessed, when his brother's words faded away.

"Yeah," Devin admitted.

"Sorry to disappoint you, but I don't have a real relationship—or any kind of relationship—with Haylee, either."

"And yet, you bought two tickets to a baseball game in Oakland despite knowing that I'd be in Montreal for the weekend."

"Maybe I forgot that you were going out of town."

"Or maybe you picked that weekend on purpose so that you'd have an excuse to offer the second ticket to Haylee…because you like her," his brother said in a teasing tone.

"Because I slept with her," he responded bluntly.

"Holy sh—" Devin clamped his jaw shut, censoring his own outburst. "You slept with Haylee Gilmore?"

"Yeah."

"After the ball game?"

He shook his head. "The night of Brielle and Caleb's wedding."

"I don't know whether to give you a high five or smack the back of your head."

"I didn't plan for it to happen," he said, aware that he sounded defensive.

"You're saying that you accidentally slept with a hot wedding guest?" his brother asked dubiously.

"I'm saying that I'm a simple guy who couldn't resist the invitation of a willing girl."

"Is that why you went to California—to see if she'd be willing again?"

"No," he said, then reconsidered. "Maybe."

"And?"

"She told me to have a safe drive back to Nevada."

Devin grinned. "Suddenly, I can't wait to meet her."

It was his fault for putting the idea in her mind, Haylee thought, as she clung to the sides of the toilet bowl late Wednesday night.

The possibility of a pregnancy hadn't even been a blip on her radar until Trevor mentioned it. But after he'd gone, she'd acknowledged—if only to herself—that her last period had not been usual. The flow had been surprisingly light and of short duration. Not that she'd given it a second thought at the time, but now she wondered...

Because it wasn't just the unusual period or even

the occasional bout of nausea, but for the past week or more, her breasts had felt heavy and tender. And she'd been tired—not just at the end of the day but first thing in the morning, hitting the snooze button rather than jumping out of bed at the sound of the alarm, as was her habit. And she knew, because she'd Googled "signs of pregnancy," that her symptoms checked too many of the boxes.

Of course, she also had a habit of scratching her head whenever she heard mention of head lice, so it was possible that the pregnancy symptoms she was experiencing were more imagined than real.

On the other hand, it was also possible that she *was* pregnant. Because she'd looked at the box of condoms after Trevor had gone and discovered that yes, they were out of date.

Way out of date.

That fact, combined with the reality of her light period, had her starting to feel a little panicky. Because having a baby wasn't anywhere in her short-term plans.

She could be happy for Josslin, because her friend was in a committed relationship and she and Rob had actually wanted to have a baby. And for Candace, because she and Derek had tried for almost three years before she finally got pregnant. And considering what her friends had been through to start their families, it seemed ridiculous to imagine that Haylee might be pregnant after the first time she'd slept with someone, especially when they'd taken precautions to avoid such an outcome.

Condoms have a shelf life.

Okay, yes, she was aware of that now. But she stubbornly refused to believe that one night with Trevor Blake had created a baby. It was far more likely that throwing up a hot dog was her stomach's way of protesting the consumption of tube meat while sitting in the sun watching a ball game.

What about the beef and green peppers with rice the following night?

Obviously her stomach was still unsettled after its rejection of the hot dog.

And the chicken parm the night after that?

Clearly her stomach had a long memory.

It couldn't be morning sickness—because she felt fine in the mornings.

Thinking it through rationally, Haylee almost managed to convince herself there was nothing to worry about. Until the next morning, when her alarm went off and she felt so exhausted she didn't want to get out of bed. Then she remembered the message she'd got from her boss the night before, asking her to meet him in his office first thing instead of heading directly to the site, and forced herself to get into gear.

She'd worked for Henry Warren for almost eight years now. The owner of Bay Electric had reluctantly taken her on as an apprentice when she was still in school—as a favor to her father, who he'd known for a lot of years. Henry had expressed more than a few doubts about her ability to succeed in the profession and was certain she'd give up long before she had the required number of hours to take her licensing exam. He'd been surprised and impressed when she graduated near the top of her class, and immediately added her to his staff.

Since then, Haylee was usually the first on-site in the morning and the last to leave at night. And she was gratified to know that her hard work and dedication were finally going to be rewarded. Right now, the crew was in the last stages on the retrofit of an old canning factory that was being converted into apartments. And when the final inspection was done, they would be moving on to another retrofit of an older and even bigger building, which Henry had promised to put Haylee in charge of because he'd be busy overseeing work at the new community center in Piedmont.

"How's the Weston project coming?" Henry asked, referring to the canning factory project by the name of the owner.

"We'll be finished today," she assured him. "The final inspection's scheduled for three o'clock tomorrow."

"That's good, because we'll need all hands on deck for the Shearing project on Monday."

"I didn't realize it was starting so soon," she said. "When did you want to meet to go over the plans? Or is that why I'm here now?"

"You're here because I wanted to tell you that Wade has the plans." Though he was speaking to her, he kept himself busy shuffling through papers on his desk to avoid meeting her gaze.

"I don't understand," she said, though she was afraid she was starting to. "Why does your nephew have the plans when you said that you were going to name me the project manager?"

"That was my intention," Henry confirmed. "But Wade's wife is pregnant again."

"What does that have to do with anything?" she asked, sincerely baffled.

"He's going to need the extra money that he'll make as project manager to support his family."

"I've worked for you longer than Wade has, and I've had my license longer," she pointed out. "I've *earned* this opportunity."

"That's all true," her boss acknowledged. "It's also true that you live in an apartment on your parents' property."

"Which is about as relevant as Wade's wife's pregnancy," she said.

"It *is* relevant," Henry insisted. "Because if I have to make cuts, at least I know I don't have to worry that you'll be homeless."

"Cuts?" she echoed, feeling numb. "Not only am I not getting the promotion you promised, but now you're telling me that I'm going to be laid off?"

"No," he denied. Then he sighed and scrubbed his hands over his face. "I mean, I hope not."

She sank down onto the edge of the chair facing his desk.

"We didn't get the community center."

"I'm sorry, Henry," she said, knowing that the loss of the contract wasn't just a blow to the company but to her boss personally.

"Me, too," he said, sounding sincerely regretful. "As soon as I've got another project, you'll be the one."

"That's what you said last time," she reminded him.

He flushed. "And I meant it. But you know Wade is my wife's sister's son and—"

"There's always a but, isn't there, Henry?"

She didn't stick around to hear his response.

Though she wanted to bury her disappointment in a pint of chocolate chip cookie dough ice cream, she still had a job to do—at least for the present.

As she made her way to the site, she found herself alternately railing against the injustice of Henry's decision and reluctantly understanding his rationale. He wasn't a bad guy. He just lived according to outdated standards and believed that Wade, being a man, needed to provide for his wife and children. Or maybe it was that Henry, being married to Wade's mom's sister, needed to keep peace in his own home.

She'd been tempted to challenge his decision, to demand to know if he might have made a different choice if she was the one who was pregnant and needed to support a child. But she knew her boss well enough to understand that he already struggled with the concept of a woman on his crew—despite her proven qualifications and competency—and the idea of a pregnant woman doing the job would be too much for him.

So it was a good thing she wasn't pregnant.

But later that day, on her way home, she stopped at the pharmacy to pick up a test.

Just to be sure.

"I really appreciate you coming early to help with the setup for the party," Brielle said, when Haylee showed up at the Circle G early the following Thursday afternoon. "When we first started planning, it seemed as if there was plenty of time to do everything that needed done, but now the party is in two days and I still have a list of errands as long as my arm."

"I'm happy to help," Haylee assured her. "And I'll no doubt be able to run your errands faster because I'm not carting a three-and-a-half-month-old baby around with me."

"It's not Colton that slows me down but all his stuff," the new mom said. "I swear, I've traveled out of the country for a week-long holiday with less than what's crammed in his diaper bag every time I walk out the door. And the bag weighs at least as much as his baby seat—with him in it."

"Just think of the biceps you'll have built up by the time he's walking," she teased.

"That might be a plus," Brie acknowledged. "And speaking of bags, where are yours?"

"I dropped them off at the Stagecoach Inn on my way over."

Her cousin's wife frowned. "I thought you were going to stay here."

Haylee shook her head. "I appreciate the invitation, really, but you've got enough going on, with the party coming up and a baby waking you at all hours of the night."

"Now we're getting to the real reason you'd rather stay at the hotel," Brie surmised.

"Actually, the real reason is that Finley had already booked the room for both of us, so when I decided to fly in early, I just bumped the check-in date forward by a few days."

"It's silly to pay for a hotel when we've got empty bedrooms here."

"Liam gave us the friends and family rate."

"I should hope so," Brie said. "But Caleb and I were

really hoping we'd get to spend more time with you, especially considering that you came all this way for our wedding and we hardly saw you that weekend."

"It was a short trip," she acknowledged. "And you were kind of busy, being the bride and all."

"I hope you had a good time at least."

"I had a great time," Haylee said. And then, as memories of that night played back in her mind, she felt the telltale flush of warm heat filling her cheeks.

"Oh. My. God." The other woman's eyes grew wide. "You hooked up with someone at the wedding."

Haylee's cheeks burned hotter. "I wouldn't call it a hookup," she denied, though of course she knew it hadn't been anything more.

"Tell me all the juicy details," Brie urged.

"There's really not much to tell." Aside from the fact that it had been the most amazing experience in her life—but of course she could hardly admit that to her cousin's wife.

"Does he live in Haven or was he an out-of-town guest?"

"He's local," she admitted.

Brie grinned. "And are you going to invite him to the anniversary party?"

"No," she immediately said again.

"Why not?"

"Because then I'd have to introduce him to my family."

"And you don't think they'd approve of him?" the other woman guessed.

"Actually, I'm more worried that they'd make a big

deal out of it. I haven't introduced them to many—" or *any* "—guys," she confided.

"As long as he's not a Blake," Brie teased.

"Why would you say that?" Haylee asked cautiously.

"Oh. My. God. He *is*."

"Would that be a problem?" she wondered, unwilling to confirm or deny the truth of the other woman's claim.

"I know you've lived your whole life in California, so you may be unaware of the history between the Blakes and the Gilmores," Brie acknowledged. "But it's been fraught with conflict."

"I've heard the stories," Haylee assured her. "I also know that the animosity between the two families is a big part of the reason that you and Caleb were apart for eight years."

Her cousin's wife nodded.

"But you're together now, and both families were there to celebrate your marriage. In fact, I heard that your grandfather made that cradle—" she nodded toward the handcrafted piece of furniture in which the baby was currently sleeping "—for Colton."

"All true," Brie agreed. "But the roots of the feud are deep in this town, and I'd hate for there to be a renewal as a result of another Blake-Gilmore romance gone wrong."

"Then you have nothing to worry about," Haylee told her. "Because there's no romance at all."

"I don't know if I'm relieved or disappointed, but I know you've somehow managed to distract me from the most important question."

"The party?" Haylee guessed.

Brie shook her head. "Which one of my Blake cousins caught your eye at the wedding?"

Chapter Eight

In addition to the multitude of errands to be done before the party, Haylee had a task of her own to complete. But first she'd have to summon enough courage to drive over to the corporate offices of Blake Mining and ask to see Trevor.

Maybe it would be better to call him and set up a meeting on neutral ground. She had his number now, though she hadn't heard from him since he'd left Oakland after the ball game. Not surprising, considering that she'd essentially shoved him out the door of her apartment that day.

So after delivering the cake topper—from the original wedding cake that Evelyn Gilmore had carefully packed and kept in a box in the attic for nearly sixty years—to Sweet Caroline's so the baker could use it on the enormous cake that had been ordered for the anniversary celebration, she intended to head over to Trevor's office. But as she exited the bakery, her empty stomach growled. Loudly.

She considered returning to the shop where there had been no shortage of tempting treats on display: cakes and cookies and muffins and doughnuts. But she knew the errands she had to run would keep her busy for much of the day—not to mention needing fuel for her conversation with Trevor—so she decided to detour to Diggers' Bar & Grill to grab something a little more substantial to eat.

And maybe she was procrastinating, too.

Putting off that inevitable meeting just a little while longer.

Or so she believed until she walked into the restaurant.

It was late for lunch, and there were several empty tables to choose from. Following the instructions on the sign to Please Seat Yourself, she started toward a narrow booth, her steps faltering when she realized Trevor was there—with a woman.

She felt a sharp pang of something that might have been disappointment and immediately chided herself for the emotional response.

She hadn't seen or heard from him in more than three weeks. Of course he hadn't been sitting around, thinking about her, and she shouldn't be surprised— never mind disappointed—that he'd obviously moved on to flirting, dating and probably even sleeping with other women.

Though she was tempted to turn back around and

walk out again, her empty stomach wouldn't allow her to retreat. Instead, she slid into the booth and picked up the laminated menu tucked behind the tray of condiments, peeking past the edge of it for a closer look at Trevor's dining companion.

It wasn't a surprise to Haylee that she was beautiful, with long blond hair that fell in loose curls to the middle of her back. She wore a sleeveless sheath-style dress in a shade of blue somewhere between royal and navy with perfectly matched high-heeled pumps on her feet. She laughed at something Trevor said, the sound neither girly nor harsh but almost musical. No doubt she was one of those women who even cried pretty, Haylee thought resentfully, all too aware that tears tended to turn her face into a splotchy red mess.

Was this a sign? she wondered. Proof that his reputation as a player was well-founded and that she should consider herself lucky that she hadn't heard from him since he'd walked out of her apartment three weeks earlier?

The server delivered Haylee's drink on her way to dropping the check at Trevor's table. His dining companion started to reach for the paper slip, but he caught her hand and shook his head, then said something that made her laugh again.

Haylee sipped her ginger ale and checked her phone for messages. There was one from Brielle, asking her to pick up an additional fifty plastic wineglasses from the party store in Battle Mountain.

She sent a quick reply, to let Brie know that she'd take care of it, then set her phone aside again.

"Haylee?"

She glanced up to find Trevor standing by her table, the blonde—even more beautiful up close—at his side. "Trevor," she said, feigning surprise. "Hi."

He didn't introduce his companion and the woman didn't offer her hand or her name, though she did smile as Trevor asked, "What are you doing here?"

"Just grabbing a quick bite before I get back to the mile-long list of errands I'm running for Brielle," she told him, playing it casual.

He grinned, and a whole kaleidoscope of butterflies spread their wings and took flight in her belly. "I meant, what brings you back to Haven this time?"

Duh. Of course that's what he meant.

"Oh. My grandparents' sixtieth wedding anniversary. They're having an open house at the Circle G to celebrate."

The blonde, apparently bored with their conversation, spoke up to say, "It sounds as if you two have things to catch up on, and I have to get back to the office." She touched her lips to Trevor's cheek. "Thanks for lunch."

"Anytime," he said.

As she walked away, Trevor slid onto the empty bench across from Haylee without waiting for an invitation.

"Don't you have to get back to work, too?" she asked.

He answered her question with one of his own. "Why does it seem as if you're always trying to get rid of me?"

"I'm not trying to get rid of you," she denied.

"Then you don't mind if I keep you company while you have your lunch?"

"I don't mind," she lied. "But your girlfriend might feel differently."

His brows drew together. "My girl—oh, you mean Jenna?"

"Is that her name?"

"It is," he confirmed. "And she's my cousin."

Her skepticism must have been evident, because he immediately offered more details, as if to convince her.

"My father's brother's daughter," he said. "And Jenna's brother, Patrick, is the owner and operator of the local Silver Star Vacation Ranch, where Brielle and Caleb had their wedding."

The server brought Haylee's soup and sandwich—and a cup of coffee for Trevor.

"Thanks, Deanna," he said.

"You're very welcome."

Haylee dipped her spoon into her soup while Trevor emptied two packages of sugar and two creamers into his cup.

"So when is this big anniversary celebration for your grandparents?"

"Saturday."

"Do you have a date?" he asked. And then, before she could respond, he continued, "Because it turns out that I'm free on Saturday."

She swallowed another mouthful of soup. "Are you angling for an invitation?"

"Actually, I'm more interested in spending time with you, but since you're going to be at the party—" he shrugged "—two birds, one stone."

"I'm going to be pretty busy, pouring drinks and serving cake, so you wouldn't really see me," she hedged. "Not to mention that the whole place is going to be overrun with Gilmores."

"You're brushing me off."

"I'm not." She nibbled on the edge of her sandwich. "I just don't want you to think that we're going to pick up where we left off."

"You mean with you throwing up and then throwing me out of your apartment?"

"No," she denied. "I meant the last time I was in Haven." But now that he mentioned it, considering how they'd parted ways that day, she was surprised that he'd want to spend time with her.

"Ahh…" His lips curved in a slow and decidedly smug smile. "You're referring to when we were naked in bed together."

She was certain the rush of color to her cheeks was answer enough that she didn't need to respond verbally.

"I'd be lying if I said I wasn't interested in the possibility of getting naked with you again," he told her. "But I wasn't presuming anything."

"Good to know," she said, and turned her attention to her sandwich.

"But since you mentioned that night…this might be a good time for me to say what I meant to say when I was in Oakland."

"What's that?" she asked, a little warily.

"That I'm sorry I didn't know it was your first time when we went back to your hotel room."

"It's all good," she said. "Really. I don't want to talk about that night."

Except that she knew they had to talk about it—not

to recap the details of their lovemaking but to discuss the repercussions of it.

Just not now. She wasn't ready to have that conversation right now.

"I just wanted you to know that if I'd known it was your first time, I would have taken more time with you."

"It's all good," she said again, silently begging him to take the hint.

Finally, he nodded.

When she'd finished eating and paid her check, Trevor walked her out to her car.

"Is your whole family going to be in town for the anniversary celebration?" he asked.

She nodded. "My dad and stepmother are driving through tomorrow, and my sister and brother are flying in Saturday morning."

"So everyone else is coming on the weekend, but you're here now," he mused.

She shrugged. "There was an unexpected lull at work, so I offered to lend a hand with some of the last-minute details."

"Hence your mile-long list of errands."

She lifted a brow. "Did you just use *hence* in a sentence?"

"Is that along the same lines as *latter*—not meaning a climbing apparatus?"

"It is," she confirmed.

"My mother made us read all the time when we were kids," he confided. "Apparently you learn things that way."

"Who knew?"

He smiled then, and though she was relieved to discover that he didn't apparently harbor any hard feelings, she knew that wasn't going to make it any easier to tell him what she needed to tell him.

"So was helping with the party really your only reason for coming to town early?" he pressed.

"You think there's another reason?"

"I do." He set his hands on her hips and moved in closer. "And I think I know what it is."

"No." As he started to lower his head toward hers, she put a hand on his chest, holding him at a distance. "You don't."

"Then tell me," he urged.

"Okay, I did come to Haven to see you," she admitted.

His lips curved, his smile just a little bit smug.

"But only because I wanted to tell you..."

"Tell me what?" he prompted, when her words trailed off.

She drew in a breath, bracing herself to say the words out loud for the very first time.

"I'm pregnant."

Trevor felt his smile slip and his stomach drop.

"What did you say?" he asked, certain he must have misheard.

"I'm pregnant," Haylee said again.

And it sounded again like she said she was pregnant, but not three weeks earlier, she'd assured him that wasn't possible. "But you said—"

"I know what I said," she interjected. "I was wrong."

He shook his head, unwilling to believe it.

This couldn't be happening to him.

Not again.

She was watching him closely, waiting for some kind of reaction or response.

"Okay," he said, and took another minute to try and organize the thoughts spinning around in his head into some semblance of order.

"You're pregnant," he finally acknowledged, because that didn't necessarily have anything to do with him. "But why are you telling me?"

"Why am I telling you?" she echoed, sounding confused. "Because it's your baby."

He swallowed the panic that was rising inside him. "Is it?"

"Are you suggesting…you think I slept with someone else?"

"I'd be an idiot not to consider the possibility that you hooked up with someone else after we were together," he told her, desperately searching for an alternative explanation to her revelation.

She drew back, as if stricken by his response. And maybe, if the widening of her eyes was sincere and not part of a deliberate deception, a little bit hurt by the accusation.

But he didn't stop there. No, despite all the warning signs of danger ahead, he forged on.

"You wouldn't be the first woman to try to trap a man with another man's baby," he said.

Now her eyes flashed with anger. "I can't tell if you have a really high opinion of yourself or a really low opinion of me."

"I'm just trying to figure out your angle," he told her.

She straightened her shoulders and lifted her chin.

"And you did," she said. "You're right. I've had several other lovers since the night we were together. So many, in fact, that I don't really have a clue who's the father of my baby, so it would probably be best if you just forgot I even said anything to you about it."

Trevor wished that he could, but the word "pregnant" was flashing like a neon sign inside his head, and he knew that forgetting wouldn't be possible.

Obviously this bombshell revelation required further discussion, but before he could think of anything to say, she was driving away.

As a result, he laid awake through the darkness of night trying to figure out what it all meant, what he was supposed to do, and with long-buried memories playing out in his mind.

"I can't be seven weeks pregnant," Alannis said to the doctor. "I got my period last month."

Dr. Perry smiled. "You wouldn't be the first expectant mom to mistake implantation bleeding for menstruation."

"Implantation bleeding?" she echoed uncertainly.

"It's what sometimes happens when the fertilized egg attaches to the lining of the uterus," the doctor explained.

"Seven weeks," Alannis said softly, her gaze on the screen showing the grainy ultrasound image of the tiny blob that would grow into their baby.

"Seven weeks and two days, to be precise."

"So the baby will be due in August?"

The doctor nodded. "August fourteenth."

But Trevor wasn't really listening anymore. He was remembering the argument he'd had with Alannis eight weeks earlier over a business trip that would require him to be out of the country for the two-year anniversary of their first date. She'd wanted to celebrate in a big way—and he knew she was hoping he'd get down on one knee—so he'd actually been relieved when his uncle had tapped him to attend the conference in Toronto.

He'd invited Alannis to go with him, thinking she might want to do some shopping or indulge in pampering at the spa, and then when he was done with work they could do some sightseeing together. But she'd turned her nose up at the invitation.

So he'd gone to the conference and she'd stayed in Haven.

She'd been waiting for him—naked in his bed—when he got back from his five-day trip, seven weeks ago today.

They'd used protection when they made love, as they always did. She'd opened the package and put the condom on him—a chore she usually disdained—and he let himself believe it was her way of apologizing for picking a fight before he went away. Or maybe a thank-you for the diamond earrings he'd brought back for her.

In any event, she'd seemed as surprised and dismayed as he when the condom broke...

And now she was seven weeks and two days pregnant.

He asked her about the date discrepancy when they left the doctor's office, but she'd waved off his questions, insisting that the doctor's estimate was only that and that she obviously couldn't be any more than seven weeks along in her pregnancy—and wasn't it exciting that they were going to have a baby?

She'd been persuasive and he'd been willing to be persuaded, and on the way home, they stopped at The Goldmine to get Alannis the ring she'd always wanted.

For the next four weeks, he'd let himself get caught up in the excitement and anticipation. Maybe he hadn't believed he was ready to settle down, but the realization that he was going to be a dad changed everything. He was happy to step up, eager to make plans for their future and the arrival of their little bundle of joy.

Then Alannis lost the baby and she blamed him, because he wasn't there for her. Because he was never there for her...

So many mistakes that he wouldn't make again.

Haylee spent Friday with her grandmother, taking her to various appointments to be primped and pampered in preparation for the big party. Of course, Evelyn Gilmore insisted on spoiling her granddaughter, too, treating her to a mani-pedi at Serenity Spa and a hair trim at Clip 'N' Curl. After that, they went to pick up the dress Evelyn had ordered from Bonnie's Boutique. The proprietor was in the process of changing the window display when they arrived, and Evelyn requested that she strip down the mannequin she'd just finished dressing so that Haylee could try the dress on.

By the time she returned to the Stagecoach Inn after dropping her grandmother off at the end of the day, Haylee was exhausted and weighted down with packages. Still, it had been a good day—and Evelyn had kept her so busy, she'd barely given Trevor Blake a passing thought.

Then she walked into the lobby and saw him.

He was dressed in a shirt and tie, as he'd been the day before, but today his tie was loosened, the top button of his shirt was undone and the cuffs of his sleeves rolled back to reveal strongly muscled forearms. His fingers jabbed at the keyboard of the laptop open on the coffee table in front of him.

She didn't know why he was there and she wasn't going to assume it was for her, so she prepared to walk by, as if she didn't even see him.

But she'd only taken a few steps when he glanced up, and he immediately jumped up to intercept her path. "I was beginning to wonder if you were ever coming back."

"Is there something you wanted? Because I think we said everything we needed to say yesterday."

"Actually, I wanted to take you for lunch."

She glanced pointedly at the oversize clock on the wall above the check-in desk. "It's four thirty."

He followed her gaze. "No wonder I'm so hungry."

Her lips twitched, but she refused to smile. She was still too angry and hurt to let herself be charmed by him.

"I've been here since eleven thirty," he confided.

"You're kidding."

"You can ask Macy if you don't believe me, but she left at three to pick up her kids and Rose came on duty. She's setting up the wine and cheese in the library now, but she can tell you that I've been here since she arrived. Thankfully, the hotel has decent Wi-Fi."

"For guests of the hotel," she pointed out.

He shrugged. "Macy gave me the password."

She set down the bags that she carried, to give her arms a momentary respite. "Why are you really here, Trevor?"

"I wanted to apologize…for the way I reacted to your news yesterday."

"Are you referring to the implication that I sleep with a different guy every weekend?"

Though her tone was cool, Trevor could see the lingering hurt in her eyes. "I didn't mean it. I know it's not true," he assured her. "But my mind was reeling and clearly not communicating with my mouth."

"I guess I can understand that," she acknowledged. "It took a long time for my head to stop spinning after I saw the plus sign on the pregnancy test."

"So what are your plans?"

"Plans?" she echoed uncertainly.

His gaze shifted away, as if he was uncomfortable asking his next question, "Are you going to have the baby?"

She tried not to react, so he wouldn't see that the question stung more than a little. After all, he didn't know her well enough to know that she would never choose to terminate a pregnancy. "Yes, I'm going to have—and keep—the baby."

"Have you seen a doctor?" he asked.

She nodded. "My family doctor confirmed the results. I have an appointment with an ob-gyn in a couple weeks."

"Let me know when and where and I'll be there."

"I didn't tell you because I expect anything from you. I just thought you had a right to know."

"And now that I know, I want to be involved."

"But that's not really practical, is it?"

"Practical or not, we need to figure out a way to make it work, because I'm going to be a part of my child's life."

Haylee wasn't sure if the words were a threat or a promise.

Chapter Nine

Having grown up in Oakland, with no extended family around, Haylee wasn't accustomed to big family gatherings. And when all of the Gilmores were together, it was a *very* big family gathering. Of course, there were other guests in attendance, too, for the celebration of her grandparents' sixtieth wedding anniversary. Friends and neighbors, young and old, and it seemed to Haylee that everyone knew everyone else. As food was eaten and beverages were drunk, groups gathered and splintered and babies were passed around.

Right now, her fourteen-year-old cousin Ashley was playing pat-a-cake with toddlers Ava, Max and Sam, while the triplets' parents enjoyed the rare opportunity to eat dinner without little ones tugging at them and demanding attention. Haylee spotted her recently engaged cousin Skylar and Skylar's fiancé, a hunky former Marine named Jake Kelly, over by the paddock with Sky's three-year-old niece Tessa, who was proudly telling everyone she met that she was getting a baby sister for Christmas. The little girl's parents, Katelyn and Reid, were setting out plates and napkins for the cutting of the cake.

"Can you watch Colton for a few minutes?" Brie asked, already passing the baby off to Haylee. "Valerie can't find her cake knife so I'm going to run home to get mine."

"Of course," she agreed, trusting that the "few minutes" wouldn't be much more than that as Caleb and Brie's house wasn't too far away on the western boundary of Circle G Ranch.

"His diaper bag's in the kitchen, if you need it, and there's a bottle in the fridge, but I fed him—" she glanced at her watch "—just about an hour ago, so—"

"Go," Haylee interjected. "Colton and I will figure things out."

"Thanks." Brie dropped a quick kiss on top of the baby's head. "Mommy will be right back."

Someone had rigged speakers up outside, and Haylee swayed from side to side with the baby along to the music. The guests of honor had been making the rounds, saying hello to all the well-wishers, when the music changed and Elvis Presley started to sing "Can't Help Falling in Love." The song must have had some significance to Jack and Evelyn, because he reached for his wife's hand and drew her into his arms. They danced right there on the grass, smiling at one another as if there was no one else around.

Watching them together, so obviously in love after sixty years together, Haylee felt her throat tighten with emotion. Their devotion to one another was a rare and precious gift, proof that happily-ever-after could happen, if only for a lucky few. Her gaze moved around the crowd, noting all the other couples in attendance.

Her dad and Colleen had been happily married for fifteen years now. (Of course, they'd only found one another after Robert Gilmore survived the implosion of his first marriage, leading Haylee to wonder if—the example of her grandparents aside—real happiness was only possible after heartbreak.) Next to her parents was her uncle Dave, also remarried after being widowed a lot of years earlier. His second wife, Valerie, was standing at his side, their hands linked together.

It was only since celebrating her twenty-ninth birthday in January and learning that various friends were getting married or having babies that Haylee had started to think about her own future and wonder if she'd ever find a partner to share her life. Not that she was in a hurry, but she'd always thought she had plenty of time. Now that she was going to have a baby, she realized that her window of opportunity wasn't only rapidly shrinking but likely already gone.

She felt a vibration against her arm and looked down at the baby in her arms, who gave her a wide, toothless grin.

"Was that gas that rumbled out of your tummy? Or did you just fill your diaper?"

Of course, he didn't respond—but the not-so-fresh scent coming from his bottom told her to prepare for the worst.

"Let's go find that diaper bag," she suggested.

It was her first time in Dave and Valerie's house, but the back door opened into a mudroom that led to the kitchen, so it didn't take her long to find the diaper bag and dig out the supplies that she needed. There was a family room off the kitchen, and she decided to change the baby in there, to afford him a little more privacy.

"It's been a lot of years since I've done this," she confided to Colton as she laid him down on the change pad. "So you might have to bear with me while I figure this out."

Of course, changing a diaper was probably the simplest of all the things she had to figure out over the next seven months or so. Messy, she acknowledged, as she wiped his bottom, but simple.

And while being a mom wasn't anything that she'd planned for this stage of her life, as she affixed the tabs on the new diaper, she already knew that she was going to love her baby more than anything.

Then she refastened the snaps on Colton's denim overalls and lifted him into her arms again.

He gurgled happily. And why wouldn't he be happy? He had a full belly, a dry diaper and a mommy and daddy who loved one another as much as they loved him.

Maybe she couldn't give her baby that kind of family, but as she tidied up the changing area, Haylee vowed to be the best mom that she could be.

Of course, she was going to have to make some compromises. She'd have to look into day care, and she wasn't sure she was comfortable with the idea of letting a stranger take care of her baby. But she was getting way ahead of herself. She had a lot of time to figure out day care—and significantly less time to figure out how and when she was going to tell her family that she was pregnant.

Maybe it would be easier if she'd ever introduced them to a boyfriend—or if the father of her baby had ever been her boyfriend. Instead, he was practically a stranger and their baby was the product of a single night together.

Yeah, she was definitely going to need some time to figure out how to explain the situation to her father. Maybe Finley would have some ideas, but she hadn't even told her sister, and as a general rule, she told her sister everything. But Finley didn't even know that she'd slept with Trevor on her previous trip to Haven, though her sister likely suspected something had happened, based on her comment about the sexual tension she'd sensed between Haylee and Trevor when he'd been at their apartment.

Of course, Finley also had no idea that Haylee had still been a virgin prior to that night with Trevor. Her always popular sister had shared all kinds of details about her romantic relationships when they were in high school, while Haylee had remained on the outside looking in. And when Haylee had headed off to college in pursuit of her liberal arts degree (which her father had insisted would help her figure out what she wanted to do and turned out to be of absolutely no other use to her as an electrician), Finley had teased her about finally having the opportunity to lose her virginity. Later she'd obviously assumed that her sister had done so at some point during her four years away, and Haylee had never corrected her mistaken assumption because she couldn't help but feel it was a little bit pathetic that she hadn't ever hooked up with anyone in all that time.

She tucked Colton's supplies back into his diaper bag.

"Are you ready to rejoin the party?" she asked him.

The baby responded with another gummy smile.

"I'll take that as a yes," she said, pushing open the door to carry him outside—and finding herself face-to-face with Trevor Blake.

He was dressed in a similar outfit to what he'd worn the night they first met, right down to the cowboy hat and boots, and her heart skipped a beat again.

His lips curved in an easy smile, then he looked from her to the baby in her arms and raised a brow. "That was fast."

"This is Colton," she told him.

"Ah, Brielle and Caleb's little guy," he realized.

She nodded.

"He's grown since the wedding."

"That was almost two months ago," she pointed out to him. But she didn't want to talk about the wedding or babies—and she especially didn't want to talk about the baby they'd made together the night of the wedding—so instead she asked, "Why are you here, Trevor?"

"I'm your date."

"I don't recall inviting you," she said. "In fact, I specifically recall *not* inviting you."

"But it occurred to me, assuming that all of these people are going to find out you're carrying my baby at some point, that it might come as less of a shock if they've actually seen us together."

"Except I wasn't planning on telling anyone that it's your baby."

"You were planning on keeping the father's identity a secret for the next seven months?"

"More like the next eighteen years," she admitted.

"Well, change of plans," he said.

"Why do you get to decide?"

"I'd prefer for us to make decisions together, but that would require you being willing to listen to my input."

"Fine," she agreed, eager to terminate the conversation before they were interrupted.

"Now that wasn't so hard, was it?" he asked, as Brielle swooped in to steal Colton out of Haylee's arms.

"And now I have my baby and my answer," she said, her gaze moving between Haylee and Trevor. And though her tone was light, her expression was worried.

"Your answer to what?" Trevor asked curiously.

"*Nothing*," Haylee said firmly, fingers mentally crossed that his cousin wouldn't say anything to reveal the subject of their previous conversation.

"Which one of my Blake cousins was most likely to crash a Gilmore party," Brie said, granting her a temporary reprieve.

"I'm not crashing," he denied. "I'm Haylee's date."

"Is that so?" Brie murmured.

"It is," Haylee confirmed, her smile tight.

"Then I'll leave you to enjoy the party," Brie said, then turned and dashed off, leaving Haylee alone with Trevor.

Trevor didn't stay long.

Just long enough to ensure everyone was talking

about the fact that he'd been there and had been very attentive to Haylee, so that when her pregnancy was revealed, people would add one plus one to come up with the requisite two—or three, adding their baby to the equation. He'd even brushed a light kiss against her lips before he left. And though she knew it was all part of his act, the fleeting touch of his mouth had stirred her up inside.

It had also stirred up a hornets' nest, as she heard several of her Gilmore relatives grumble about "those damn Blakes"—conveniently forgetting, or maybe not caring, that they'd recently danced at the wedding of a Gilmore and a Blake.

Of course, when she got back to the hotel room she was now sharing with her sister, Finley had wanted to know all the details about what she believed was a blossoming romance between her sister and the week-end cowboy. And the late night meant that Haylee was dragging the next morning.

"I'm going to run over to The Daily Grind to grab a latte and a cruller," Finley said, when Haylee got out of the shower. "What can I get for you?"

Haylee considered as she rubbed a towel over her wet hair.

"A chocolate glazed," she decided, her mouth watering at the prospect of biting into the sweet treat. Her stomach, though, seemed a little uneasy about the fried dough. "On second thought, change the doughnut to peppermint tea."

"Are you okay?" Finley asked, concerned.

"Yeah. I just haven't completely bounced back from that stomach bug I had." Which, of course, hadn't really been a stomach bug at all but merely the explanation she'd given her sister to explain why she'd had her head in the toilet.

Her sister frowned. "That was three weeks ago."

"I know."

"And you're still not feeling one hundred percent?"

"I'm feeling a lot better," she said. "I'm just not sure I'm ready for a doughnut, but tea sounds good."

"Tea instead of coffee? I'm stunned."

"I think I OD'd on caffeine yesterday," she fibbed. "I'm still feeling a little jittery."

"Okay, tea it is," Finley said with a shrug.

Haylee exhaled a sigh of relief when her sister had gone. Though Finley had mostly accepted the excuses and explanations she'd offered for her queasiness, tiredness and recent dietary changes, she knew she wouldn't be able to keep her pregnancy a secret for very much longer. And it wasn't really that she wanted to keep it a secret so much as she needed to figure things out on her own before everyone else started chiming in with well-meaning advice.

She busied herself packing while her sister was out, eager to get on the road to the airport when Finley returned. She was just zipping up her suitcase when a knock sounded at the door.

Assuming her sister couldn't get to her key because her hands were full, she automatically pulled opened the door—and found herself face-to-face with Trevor again.

"This is getting to be a habit," she said.

"Good morning to you, too," he said cheerily.

"Sorry—I got a late start this morning and I have to finish packing before Finley gets back."

"Packing?" He frowned. "Where are you going?"

"Home."

"You can't go back to California," he protested. "You're having my baby."

"Baby?" Finley echoed from the hallway.

Haylee looked past the man to her sister standing on the other side of the open door with a takeout bag and tray of hot drinks in her hands and her jaw on the floor.

She glared at Trevor, furious that he'd outed their secret to her sister without any preparation or warning.

"Oh. My. God." Finley pushed past him into the room. She set the tray and bag on the dresser and turned to face her sister, hands on her hips. "You didn't have a stomach bug, did you? You're pregnant."

"Yes, I'm pregnant," she admitted.

"Why didn't you tell me?" her sister demanded, sounding hurt.

"I didn't tell anyone until I told Trevor, three days ago."

"You should have told *me*," Finley insisted.

"You're right, and I'm sorry," Haylee said, attempting to appease her. "And you can yell at me all you want later, but right now, can you give us a few minutes?"

"Five minutes," Finley reluctantly agreed.

"Thank you."

Trevor didn't waste any time. As soon as the door had closed behind her sister, he said, "I think we should get married."

Haylee stared at him as though he'd grown a second head. "You've got to be kidding me."

"I'm not," he assured her.

"Aren't you the same man who bluntly told me, only three weeks ago, that you wouldn't marry me?"

"Because I had no intention of being trapped into marriage, if that was your endgame when you invited me back to your room."

"I didn't have an endgame. There was no plan to seduce you—or anyone—when I came to Haven for the wedding. In fact, I didn't even want to come."

"That's all water under the bridge," he said. "What matters now is moving forward."

"And how are we supposed to do that?"

"You could start by responding to my proposal."

"I'm not sure 'we should get married' counts as a proposal," she remarked dryly. "And even if it does, my answer is *no*."

He scowled. "What do you mean, *no*?"

"I mean that I'm not going to marry you."

"But…you're pregnant with my baby," he said again.

"Maybe you should put a billboard up on Main Street to ensure everyone in town knows."

"I haven't told anyone—aside from your sister," he said.

"That's exactly my point," she said.

"You weren't planning to tell her?"

"Yes, *I* was planning to tell her. When *I* was ready."

"I'm sorry," he said, sounding sincerely regretful. "But I bet all would be forgiven if you asked her to be your maid of honor at our wedding."

Haylee shook her head. "Do you even listen when other people talk?"

"Getting married is the right thing to do."

"Says who?" she challenged.

"Says me."

"Well, I don't happen to think that an unplanned pregnancy is a good reason to exchange vows," she argued.

He folded his arms over his chest. "Can you think of a better reason?"

Love, she wanted to say.

But, of course, they weren't in love. They'd shared nothing more than a moment of lust and now they were dealing with the consequences of that weakness.

She mentally winced at the thought, refusing to think of her pregnancy as a punishment. Maybe she wouldn't have chosen to have a baby right now—or with a guy she barely knew—but she regretted only the circumstances of her child's conception, not the tiny being growing inside her.

"Obviously you need some time to think about my proposal," he decided.

She huffed out a breath. "I don't need time—I need you to go away."

"Then I guess neither one of us is going to get what we want," he told her.

Haylee knew that her sister would have questions. She also knew that Finley would respect her desire to keep the news of her pregnancy quiet and not ask those questions in front of Logan, and since they were all flying back to Oakland together, she had a few more hours to sort out her thoughts before the interrogation began.

Or so she believed until Logan's flirtation with the airline attendant at the check-in counter resulted in him being upgraded to first class—leaving his sisters in coach with no barrier between them. She did, however, wait until the beverage service had passed their row before she began.

"When I asked you why you were stress baking, three weeks after Caleb and Brielle's wedding, you told me that you'd *met* somebody there," Finley said, sounding hurt. "You never told me that you'd *slept* with him."

"I didn't know how to tell you," Haylee said.

"How about—'Hey, Fin. I met this really hot guy and banged his brains out'?"

Heat crept up Haylee's neck and into her cheeks. "I'll try to remember that for next time, but it was a first for me."

"What was a first? Sleeping with someone you just met—or having a one night stand?"

"Both," Haylee admitted.

It was a simple one-word answer, but something in her tone must have given her away, because Finley's gaze narrowed suspiciously. "But you'd had sex before, right?"

"Not…no," she admitted.

Her sister looked stunned. Her mouth opened and then closed again before she finally asked, "What did you do when you were at college?" Then she shook her head. "Never mind. Obviously nothing worth talking about."

"And that's why I didn't tell you," Haylee said. "It was embarrassing enough to be a twenty-nine-year-old virgin without having to confess that fact to my much more beautiful and ever popular sister."

"I'm not more beautiful," Finley denied. "And I was only more popular because I was more outgoing. People asked me to go out and do things because I said yes—I didn't realize it was an issue for you."

"Of course it was an issue," she said. "How could it not be an issue when every boy I ever liked in high school liked you better?

"And maybe that's why I didn't say anything about what happened with Trevor," she admitted now. "Because deep down inside, I knew it wouldn't have happened—he wouldn't have looked at me twice—if you'd been there."

"If you really believe that, you haven't been paying attention when the guy looks at you," Finley said.

"He only looks at me because I'm pregnant with his baby."

"Did he know that when he was in Oakland?"

"*I* didn't even know it then."

"Which proves my point," Finley said smugly.

Haylee didn't think it proved anything—and she had more pressing concerns anyway. "What am I supposed to do?"

"What do you want to do?"

She sighed. "Travel back in time two months and buy a new box of condoms."

"You do know there are options…"

"I know," she said. "But I do want the baby—that's the one thing I do know. But I'm scared, too, and I can't help wondering what if…"

"What if you change your mind about wanting your child—like mom did about us?" Finley guessed.

"Yeah," Haylee admitted. "Maybe there's some kind of maternal deficiency in her genes—and maybe I've got it, too."

"Or maybe Sandra Burke is just a selfish woman who wanted more than the life she had with our dad," her sister suggested as an alternative. "After all, she hasn't abandoned Sebastian," she added, referring to their half brother from their mother's second marriage.

Haylee considered that as she nibbled the complimentary pretzels and sipped her ginger ale.

After a few minutes, Finley spoke again, saying gently, "I'm sorry."

"Why are *you* sorry?" Haylee asked.

"I was upset because I thought you were holding out on me, but I realize now that you were dealing with a boatload of stuff. I still wish you'd confided in me rather than dealing with it alone, but I can understand that the whole situation must have seemed overwhelming."

"I'm sorry, too," Haylee said now. "You've always been there for me and I shouldn't have expected that this time would be any different."

"Thank you," her sister said.

"And I promise, the next time I'm dealing with a boatload of stuff, I'm dragging you onboard with me."

Finley nudged her arm. "I'll be the one with the life jackets."

Because she'd always been there to buoy her sister's spirits, and Haylee knew that she always would be.

Trevor was scowling at the papers on his desk when his brother walked into his office Monday morning.

"Hazel warned me that you were in a mood," Devin said from the doorway.

"Even happy is a mood," he noted.

"Which you are clearly not."

"I've just got a lot on my mind."

"A lot—or a woman?" his brother queried.

Trevor ignored the question to ask one of his own. "Why are you here? You always say you like doing tech support for the company because you can do it from home."

"Most of the time that's true, but there was a hardware issue I had to look into and I thought I'd stop by to see if you wanted to grab coffee before I head out."

"Sure, coffee sounds good," Trevor decided, since he wasn't able to concentrate on much of anything anyway.

"The Daily Grind or Sweet Caroline's?"

"Tough choice," he admitted. The Daily Grind had better coffee, but Sweet Caroline's had the best pastries.

They opted for Sweet Caroline's, because it was a little closer to the office.

"I meant to tell you—I met Haylee Gilmore here Saturday morning," Devin said, when they were seated with their drinks and sweets—a chocolate croissant for Trevor and cherry Danish for Devin.

"She was in town for her grandparents' sixtieth anniversary celebration on the weekend," Trevor said.

"That would explain the huge cake that I helped load into her car," his brother noted. "So...you knew she was here?"

He nodded. "I ran into her at Diggers' on Thursday. And at the hotel on Friday."

"What were you doing at the hotel?" Devin wondered.

"Waiting for Haylee," he admitted.

"You turning into a stalker?" his brother asked worriedly.

He scowled. "Of course not. I'm just trying to figure out how to convince her to marry me."

Devin choked on his coffee. "You want to marry her?"

"I'm going to marry her," he clarified.

"But you've known her all of—" his brother did a quick calculation his head "—eight weeks. And for most of those weeks, she's been in California." Then realization dawned. "She's pregnant, isn't she?"

He nodded. "And before you say anything else, let me assure you that I learned my lesson about the dangers of unprotected sex a long time ago, but apparently the disclaimer on the condom box is there for a valid reason."

Devin considered this for a long minute before asking, "You're sure it's your—"

"I'm sure," he cut in. He might have implied otherwise to Haylee, but that had been a knee-jerk reaction borne of panic. When he was able to think clearly again, he'd known there was no way she'd lost her virginity to him the night of the wedding and then taken another lover a short while later.

"Wow." Devin cleared his throat. "I'm not quite sure what else to say."

"'Wow' about sums it up," Trevor acknowledged.

"You don't seem to be freaking out," his brother noted.

"I freaked out when she told me."

"A reasonable reaction under the circumstances, I'd say." Devin swallowed a mouthful of coffee, then mused, "So…you're going to be a dad."

Trevor's fingers tightened on the handle of his mug. "That's the plan."

His brother cursed, belatedly remembering that Trevor had been down this same road once before. "Damn. Sorry."

"No need to be," he said. "But I will ask you to keep this to yourself. It's early days yet and Haylee isn't ready to share the news."

"Of course," Devin agreed. "But you said something about needing to convince Haylee to marry you—are you telling me that you proposed and she said no?"

He nodded.

Devin started to chuckle, then faked a cough to cover it up.

"I'm glad you're amused," Trevor remarked dryly. "But I fail to see any humor in the situation."

"Of course you do," his brother acknowledged. "Because you're so accustomed to women falling at your feet that you don't know how to woo one."

"Woo one?" Trevor echoed, shaking his head. "Jesus, Dev. No one talks like that anymore."

His brother just shrugged. "Maybe that's the problem. Wooing a woman has become a lost art."

"And what do you know about wooing women?" he challenged.

"A fair amount, I'd say, after having read extensively on the subject."

Trevor resisted the urge to roll his eyes. "And has all that knowledge actually gotten you a date?"

"It will, when I find the right woman," Devin insisted.

"The world is full of women. How will you know the right one if you don't go out with any of them?" he asked.

"Is Haylee the right one for you?"

"She's having my baby," he reminded his brother.

"And that's why she turned down your proposal," Devin deduced.

Trevor frowned. "What's why?"

"You don't want to marry Haylee. You only want to do the right thing."

It was exactly what Haylee had said, and he was a little uncomfortable to realize that his motivation was so obvious.

"Not five minutes ago, you seemed to agree that I should marry her," he reminded his brother.

"But she has to *want* to marry you," Devin said. "Which means that you need to take action and not just rely on the fact that you're Trevor Blake and any woman should feel lucky to wear your ring on her finger."

"I think taking action is what got us into this situation."

"Try to think outside the bedroom," Devin suggested dryly.

Trevor knew that he should heed his brother's advice, but he couldn't help thinking that even if seducing Haylee wasn't guaranteed to get her on board with his marriage plan, it would certainly be enjoyable.

Chapter Ten

Haylee booked half a day off work for a dental appointment the Thursday after the anniversary party. Though it was only a little white lie, she still felt guilty about the deception. Not that she believed she owed her boss the truth, but her family was a different matter.

Several of the online resources she'd consulted had noted that many expectant women chose not to share their happy news until after the first trimester because of the fifteen to twenty-five percent of pregnancies that ended in miscarriage, eighty percent of those happened within the first three months. And despite her pregnancy being unplanned, she knew she'd be devastated if anything happened to her baby.

She also knew it wasn't fear of losing her baby that

was the reason for her silence—it was fear of her father's disappointment and disapproval.

Finley had been surprisingly silent on the subject of her sister's pregnancy since their return from Haven. Though Haylee suspected there was much she wanted to say, so far she'd kept her opinions to herself.

As the date of her ob-gyn appointment drew nearer, she considered asking Finley to go with her. Partly to show her sister that she'd never intended to exclude her and partly because she was a little nervous about going on her own. In the end, though, she decided not to say anything, because she didn't want to put Finley in the position of keeping any more information from the rest of the family.

The only person who knew of her plans was Trevor. Since her return from Haven, he'd kept in not just regular but frequent communication. They talked almost daily and exchanged text messages even more often. She was surprised to realize that she enjoyed their conversations and actually looked forward to chatting with him every day.

Maybe because the distance allowed her to talk to him as the father of her baby and forget that she melted into a puddle of hormones whenever she was in close proximity to him. But they didn't only talk about her pregnancy—they talked about all manner of topics, the kind of getting-to-know-one-another conversations that usually happened on first and second dates—before a man and woman ended up in bed together.

During their conversation a few days earlier, Haylee had told him about her appointment. He'd asked her about the when and where, but she hadn't expected him to make note of the details. But now it was Thursday at one o'clock, and he was standing at her door.

"Is there another baseball game today?" she asked, ignoring the way her heart bumped against her ribs.

He grinned, as if he could see right through her feigned indifference—and maybe he could.

"As a matter of fact, there is," he said. "The A's are playing in Kansas City today."

"Then you obviously made a wrong turn somewhere."

He shrugged. "Since I did, maybe you wouldn't mind if I went to see the doctor with you?"

"I don't mind," she allowed. "But I didn't expect that you'd actually come all this way for a prenatal checkup."

"It's my baby, too," he said.

"I'm not likely to forget that fact," she assured him.

"And, as I told you before, I want to be involved in my child's life."

"I assumed that meant *after* the baby was born," she admitted.

"Maybe I want to be there for you, too."

Her gaze narrowed suspiciously. "Why?"

"Because I know you haven't told anyone else about your pregnancy, aside from your sister—"

"Actually, *you* told my sister."

"—and I didn't want you to have to go through this on your own," he continued, ignoring her interjection.

It was a sweet—and surprising—gesture. And not an impulsive one. Working for a family-owned business, he obviously had a great deal of flexibility, but she'd never anticipated that he'd travel so far to take her to a doctor's appointment.

"So…are you ready to go?"

"The appointment isn't until three o'clock," she reminded him.

"Great. That means we have time for lunch first."

Haylee had been prepared to go to the clinic on her own, but she was glad Trevor was there. Maybe their relationship was untraditional—if it could even be called a relationship—but despite having been taken aback by the news of her pregnancy, he'd stepped up.

She'd been admittedly skeptical when he'd told her that he would be there for her and the baby. It seemed like a lot of talk from a man who lived in a different state, but now he was here, proving that he was willing to make the effort.

"Hi, Haylee." The doctor offered her hand and a warm smile when she walked into the exam room. "I'm Kelly Robertson."

"It's nice to meet you," Haylee said.

"I see you brought a friend," the doctor noted, glancing at the man standing beside her patient.

"Trevor Blake," he said, shaking her hand in turn. "I'm the baby's father."

"I'm glad you're here," Dr. Robertson said. "It's always easier for the expectant mom if she has support during her pregnancy—and after, of course."

"Trevor lives in Nevada," Haylee felt compelled to point out.

"He should get bonus points then, for coming all this way for a prenatal checkup."

"You hear that?" Trevor nudged his shoulder against hers. "I should get bonus points."

Haylee rolled her eyes as the doctor chuckled.

"Of course, it's the expectant mom who has to do all the really hard work," Dr. Robertson said, "so we're going to focus on her right now."

She turned to Haylee and continued. "Today, we're going to check your vital signs—heart rate, breathing and blood pressure, which we'll continue to monitor throughout your pregnancy. We're going to review your personal and family medical history, talk about your menstrual cycle, birth control usage and reproductive history. Then we're going to conduct a physical exam, calculate your estimated due date, and confirm the date with an ultrasound scan, which will also give you a first peek at your baby. Any questions about any of that?"

Haylee shook her head.

"Having the dad here means we can get his family medical history, too," the doctor said. "But I will ask him to step out of the room while you have your physical exam and invite him to come back for the ultrasound, okay?"

"Okay," she agreed.

Trevor nodded.

"Great." She reached for a blood pressure cuff. "Let's get started."

The doctor asked a steady stream of questions and made notes directly into the computer on her desk as she went along.

"Any abdominal pain, nausea or vomiting?"

"I've had some morning sickness," Haylee acknowledged.

"But not just in the morning," Trevor chimed in.

"I know it can be disruptive and unpleasant, but

it will pass," the doctor promised. "Though it varies from one expectant mother to the next—and even from one pregnancy to the next—it generally starts to let up around week ten and is usually resolved by week fourteen.

"In the meantime, I'd advise eating smaller meals more frequently and sticking to bland foods as much as possible. And if you lose a few pounds in the first trimester, don't panic—you'll gain them back again soon enough."

"What if I'm throwing up but still gaining weight?" Haylee asked. Most of the articles she'd read on pregnancy suggested that a lot of expectant moms lost weight in the first trimester, but despite the intense—and thankfully short-lived—bouts of nausea, her appetite had returned and her clothes were already starting to feel snug.

"That's less common but not an obvious cause for concern, either, especially for a mom who's young and healthy and fit," Dr. Robertson said. "Do you feel as if you've put on a couple extra pounds?"

She nodded. "Four pounds."

The doctor smiled but made a note in the computer.

She asked Trevor to step outside while she performed the physical exam, but invited him back in again for the ultrasound, so that they could actually see their baby.

"Are you nervous?" he asked, as they waited for the doctor to return with the portable scan machine.

"Nervous and scared," she admitted. "And maybe just a little bit excited."

He took her hand and linked their fingers together.

It felt like an oddly intimate act, despite the fact that

their bodies had been joined even more intimately, but she held on, grateful for his presence.

"How about you?" she asked.

"I'm flat-out terrified," he admitted.

"Why are *you* terrified? There isn't a baby growing inside you, getting ready to push all your internal organs out of place."

He winced at the thought. "I'm terrified because, up until this point, this has been more of a concept than a reality—for me," he acknowledged. "Seeing our baby will make everything real."

"I'm the one who decided to have this baby," she reminded him. "You don't have to stick around if it's not what you want."

"You want to have and raise a baby on your own?" His tone was skeptical.

"It wouldn't be my first choice, but getting pregnant by the first guy I ever slept with wasn't a lifelong ambition, either."

"Maybe it was meant to be," he said.

"You don't believe that," she chided.

"I'm not sure what I believe anymore, but I do want to stick around. I want to be there for you and our baby."

He sounded sincere, and the fact that he was here certainly added weight to his claim, but it was early days yet. The prospect of parenthood was novel, maybe even exciting. But how long would it hold his attention? What would happen when he started to date someone who objected to him spending time with the woman who was pregnant with his child? And what would it mean for their child when he decided to start a family with someone else? Would their child be neglected? Forgotten?

"Haylee…"

"Yeah?"

"You're cutting off the circulation in my fingers."

"What? Oh." She immediately loosened her grip. "Sorry."

"Maybe you're a little bit scared, too," he suggested.

She was, but not for the reasons he assumed. She was afraid of making the same mistakes her parents had made—and of her child paying the price.

The brisk tap on the door cut off this uncomfortable introspection.

"Are you ready for the fun part?" Dr. Robertson asked, as she wheeled the portable machine into the room.

"Ready," Haylee confirmed.

"That's the spirit." The doctor took a seat on the swiveling stool and tapped a few keys on the computer. "Dad, why don't you stand behind Mom so that you can see what's happening?"

Trevor obediently moved to the other side of the table.

The doctor peeled back the paper sheet over Haylee's abdomen and took a bottle of gel from the warming tray, squirting it on the expectant mom's belly.

"I just need to take some measurements first, to help verify your estimated due date, and then we'll let you take a peek at your little one," she promised.

"Shouldn't my due date be thirty-eight weeks after the date of conception?" Haylee asked.

"It should," the doctor agreed. "But unless a woman

is tracking her ovulation, it's not possible to accurately pinpoint the date of conception. And even if there's a specific event—an oops, we forgot birth control or the condom broke—there's no way to be certain that ovulation and fertilization coincided on that date. Because the egg might only be viable between twelve and twenty-four hours, but a woman can get pregnant from an act of intercourse occurring up to five days prior to ovulation and even two days after."

"I didn't realize there were so many variables," Haylee admitted.

"Believe it or not, ultrasound measurement of the fetus in the first trimester is the most accurate method to establish gestational age."

"In that case, I'll stop talking and let you get to it."

Dr. Robertson chuckled as she began to move the wand over the patient's abdomen. "I'm happy to answer any and all questions that either of you might have, at any time... Oh, this is a surprise."

Haylee squeezed Trevor's hand tighter. "What do you mean? Is something wrong with the baby?"

"No, nothing's wrong," the doctor hastened to assure them. "Everything looks good... Here, why don't I let you take a closer look at this." She turned the monitor so they could see what she was looking at. "As I was saying, everything looks good—" she smiled then "—with both babies."

"I'm sorry—*what*?"

"There's the first baby—" Dr. Robertson pointed to a small blob on the screen, then moved the wand and her finger "—and there's the second one."

"Two babies?" Trevor said, sounding stunned.

"Twins?" Haylee said at the same time, in a similar tone.

"Twins," the doctor confirmed.

Trevor didn't remember much of what happened after that.

The doctor continued to do her thing, but he couldn't really focus on anything she'd said after confirming that Haylee was pregnant with twins.

Due March 25. Somehow the date had penetrated the fog that had descended on his brain. And the warning that it wasn't unusual for multiples to come early. Which meant that he and Haylee had less than six-and-a-half months to get ready for the arrival of two babies.

Two babies.

He glanced at Haylee as they exited the clinic.

She appeared as shell-shocked as he felt.

"Do you want to sit down?" he asked. "You look like you're going to pass out."

"I'm fine. I'm just…" She lowered herself onto the edge of one of the benches that flanked the doors. "I guess my head is spinning a little."

"Mine, too," he admitted.

"I'm not sure I'd completely wrapped my head around the idea of one baby and now…"

He nodded his agreement.

"Twins." She tipped her head to look up at him, her expression just a little bit panicked. "What am I going to do?"

He sat down beside her. "I think you mean, what are *we* going to do?"

"I figured you'd be on your way back to Haven—as fast as possible."

"The thought did cross my mind," he confided. Then he shrugged. "But you know where I live."

She managed a smile, but it wobbled around the edges and her eyes filled with tears.

"Obviously this changes things," he said.

She nodded slowly.

"Now there are twice as many reasons to get married."

"Still not good reasons," she argued.

"Twice as many midnight feedings and dirty diapers," he pointed out.

She closed her eyes. "Thanks. You're helping me feel so much better."

"I'm trying to help you see that we need to do this together."

"How are we supposed to do anything together when we live five hundred miles apart?"

"You could move to Haven and move in with me," he suggested.

"That's a great idea," she said, her voice dripping with sarcasm. "Except that my job and my family—*my entire life*—is in Oakland."

"You want me to move here?"

"No!" Then, in a curious tone, she asked, "Would you?"

He shrugged. "I'm willing to consider all options, including the most obvious solution to this situation— marriage," he added, in case it wasn't obvious.

"Marriage only seems like the obvious solution right now," she said. "But a legal union based on a shaky foundation is destined to fail, and then we'd end up fighting over custody and access and a wagon wheel Roy Rogers garage sale coffee table."

He looked at her blankly. "A *what kind* of coffee table?"

"See?" she said. "That proves it. If you knew me, you'd know that *When Harry Met Sally* is my favorite movie."

"If you move to Haven—or I move here, we'll have plenty of time to get to know one another," he pointed out. "And even watch cheesy movies together."

"It's not a cheesy movie," she denied. "It's a classic."

"*Casablanca* is a classic," he told her.

She narrowed her gaze. "Are you sure you haven't seen *When Harry Met Sally*?"

"I don't think so, but I'd be happy to watch it if it means that much to you."

She closed her eyes then and sighed. "What are we going to do?"

"We don't need to make any decisions right now," he reassured her. "What we need is ice cream."

Haylee offered a tremulous smile. "You read my mind."

Trevor went back to Haven that night, but he called Haylee the next day, just to check in. And again the day after that, to see how she was doing. Their phone conversations had already become a regular part of her nightly routine, and it was one she looked forward to.

But when he called the following Wednesday night, she was tempted not to answer because she knew he'd immediately suspect something was wrong and she wasn't ready to talk about it. So she let his first call go to voice mail, and the second one, too.

Next came a text message:

If you don't answer your phone, I'm going to call emergency services to request a welfare check.

The third time he called, she answered.

"What's going on?" he asked, immediately concerned.

"I'm just feeling a little overwhelmed about everything."

"I'd say that's understandable, considering the recent revelation that you're going to have two babies in about six months," he noted.

"True," she agreed. And maybe she should have left it at that, but he'd proven to be a really good listener and, since Finley was out, she really needed someone to talk to right now. "But it's not only the pregnancy."

"Is there anything I can do to help?"

The sincere concern in his voice nearly undid her, but she drew in a deep breath and slowly let it out again, determined to hold it together—to pretend her whole life wasn't falling apart. "Do you know anyone who's looking to hire an electrician?"

"What? Why?"

She sniffled. "I kind of lost my job today."

"Because you're pregnant?" he guessed.

She shook her head, then realized he couldn't see her. "No. I didn't even have a chance to tell my boss the news before he called me into his office to explain that the company was experiencing an unexpected downturn and there wasn't enough work to keep everyone on."

"I'm sorry, Haylee."

"I'm not even the most junior employee, but I was the first one to get cut." And though she could probably make a case that she was let go because she was a woman, in violation of California labor laws, what would be the point?

"Did you lose your medical insurance, too?"

She groaned softly. "I didn't even think about that."

"I'll have you added to my plan," he promised.

She knew the out-of-pocket costs for prenatal care and hospital delivery could be daunting, so it would be foolish to refuse. "Can you do that?"

"It would be easier if we were married," he said. "But yes, I can and I will."

"Thank you," she said sincerely.

"But since you've got some time on your hands, why don't you come back to Haven for a while?"

"Do you have any rewiring that you need done?"

He chuckled. "Unfortunately, no. But I did hear that the mayor was putting out a tender for someone to do the holiday installations."

"For real?" she asked, her curiosity piqued.

"For real," he assured her. "Terry James has been lighting up Main Street for the past thirty-five years, but he and his wife retired to Arizona in May and apparently nobody gave a passing thought to who might take over the work he usually did."

"There can't only be one electrician in town," she said.

"Of course not," he agreed. "But Sparky is busy with

the new housing development and most of his guys are already working overtime there."

"There's an electrician in town whose name is Sparky?"

"It's a nickname—if not an original one," he told her. "His real name is Rohan. I went to school with his younger brother, so I could use that connection to reach out and ask if he's hiring and then pass your information along, if you think you might be interested in a change of scenery for a few weeks."

"I can't imagine twiddling my thumbs until Henry calls me back," she said. "And I've worked on holiday installations in the past."

"Is that a yes?"

"Yes," she said. After all, there was no harm in getting more details. A decision about the job wouldn't have to be made until it was actually offered to her.

"I'll call Sparky first thing in the morning," he promised.

"Thanks." She knew there were no guarantees, that Sparky might be as reluctant to hire a woman as Henry had initially been. But if he was willing to take a chance on her, it might not be a bad idea to get out of Oakland for a while—or at least until she figured out how to tell her father that he was going to be a grandfather.

Chapter Eleven

Sparky was more than happy to look at Haylee's résumé and, after a brief telephone interview confirmed that she was eligible to work in Nevada, he offered her an eight-week contract to help with the town's holiday lighting and, in his words, "get the mayor off my back."

Three days later, she said a tearful goodbye to her family and was on her way to Haven.

Her sister had packed a cooler with healthy snacks and drinks, probably not so much for Haylee as for the babies. Finley had been thrilled to learn that she would have not just one but two babies to cuddle and spoil before the end of March, and she was practically bursting to share the news with someone—anyone. But Haylee knew she could trust her sister to keep her secret.

She was driving to Nevada this time, so that she

wouldn't have to rent a vehicle when she got there. Driving also meant that if she decided this was a bad idea while she was en route, she had the option of turning around—as she considered doing every sixty minutes or one hundred miles—whichever came first.

She didn't have any concerns about the job she would be doing—she was looking forward to the opportunity to be busy and productive again. No, it was the proximity to Trevor that worried her.

Not that she was going to move in with him. He'd immediately offered, assuring her that he had plenty of space, but she'd declined. Not just because it would raise the eyebrows of every Gilmore and Blake in Haven, or even because she didn't want news of such an arrangement to make its way back to her father, but because she didn't trust herself not to fall under Trevor Blake's spell.

In any event, when word got around that she would be working temporarily in Haven, Haylee fielded several calls from family members with offers of empty rooms. She accepted Caleb and Brielle's offer.

"This is great," Haylee said, turning around in the middle of the spacious and beautifully decorated guest room. "I don't know how I can ever thank you guys enough."

"You might not be so thankful when Colton wakes you up several times in the middle of the night," Brie warned.

"I'm happy to help with the baby in any way that I can."

"We'll see if you're so willing at 3:00 a.m.," Caleb said dryly.

"We'll see if I hear him," Haylee said. "I'm a pretty deep sleeper."

"Colton's screams could wake the dead."

"Stop that," Brie scolded her husband. "You're going to have her calling the Stagecoach Inn for a room before she's even unpacked."

"Here's a better idea," Caleb suggested, grabbing his wife around the waist and nuzzling her throat. "We'll let Haylee stay with the banshee baby and we'll get a room at the hotel."

"Now that's a tempting proposition," Brie agreed. "Regan said the Wild Bill suite was incredible."

"Make the reservation," Haylee said. "Me and Colton can hang for a weekend while you get busy making him a little brother or sister."

"Oh no," her cousin immediately protested. "No way."

"He means 'not yet,'" Brie said.

"Could you imagine?" Caleb asked his wife. "If you got pregnant now, we'd have another baby not long after Colton's first birthday. It would almost be like having twins." He shuddered at the thought.

"My sister and her husband have twin girls," Brie explained to Haylee. "They're absolutely adorable, but there's no denying that Regan and Connor have their hands full."

Haylee managed a stiff smile. "I can't imagine."

"I don't want to," Caleb said. "Now, if you don't need me for anything else here, I'm going to head out to feed the horses."

"Go ahead," Brie said. "I'll keep Haylee company while she unpacks."

Her husband nodded. "I won't be long."

But still he brushed a soft, lingering kiss on his wife's lips before he slipped out the door.

"Married eight years and you still act like newly-weds," Haylee teased.

Her cousin's wife laughed. "Maybe the secret to keeping the romance alive is living apart for the first seven-and-a-half of those years."

"I think the secret is love," Haylee said, a little wistfully. "That's obviously what brought you back to one another after so much time apart."

"It was love—and a little bit of luck."

"Luck?"

"I guess you haven't heard the whole story," Brie said.

And while Haylee transferred her clothes from suitcase to dresser, the other woman told her about her chance encounter with Caleb at a hotel in Vegas during a girls' weekend getaway and how her impulsive decision to spend one last night with the only man she'd ever loved had created not only their son but their second chance.

"So how far along are you?" Brie asked, as Haylee zipped up her empty suitcase after her packing was undone.

"What?"

"I just had a baby," Brie reminded her. "I'm familiar with the early signs of pregnancy."

Haylee sighed and sank onto the edge of the mattress. "Ten weeks. But you have to promise not to tell *anyone*. I'm still trying to figure out how to tell my parents."

"Of course. Wait, is that why you wanted to get away

from Oakland for a while?" Brie asked, sounding concerned. "Because you haven't told the father, either?"

"No. The father knows," Haylee said. "But…he isn't in Oakland. He's here."

"Oh." The other woman obviously put enough pieces together then to see the big picture, because her eyes went wide. *"Oh."*

Haylee nodded.

"Just when the dust was starting to settle," Brie mused. "How did Trevor react to the news?"

"He was understandably surprised," Haylee said. "Because we were impulsive but not careless."

"I know he has a reputation as a player," Brie said. "But I hope you won't judge him for it. I think he deliberately cultivated that persona because he didn't want people feeling sorry for him."

"Why would anyone feel sorry for him?" Haylee wondered.

Trevor's cousin hesitated, as if she was uncertain about how much to say—or had perhaps already said too much.

"Come on, Brie, he's handsome and popular and a Blake—why would anyone feel sorry for him?" she asked again.

"Because he was engaged a few years ago," Brie finally confided. "And…his fiancée was pregnant."

She swallowed. "What happened?"

"She lost the baby."

Haylee's eyes filled with tears. "I can't imagine how horrible that must have been for both of them."

Trevor's cousin nodded. "And made even worse by the fact that Alannis blamed Trevor."

"Why?" she wondered, her heart aching for his loss.

"Because he wasn't there when it happened. And so of course he blamed himself, too."

"How long ago was this?"

"I was living in New York at the time, but I think it was four—or maybe five—years ago," Brielle said. "They broke up a short while later and, as far as I know, he hasn't been in a serious or exclusive relationship since then."

"Well, our relationship is neither serious nor exclusive—if it can even be called a relationship," Haylee said.

"I'll bet he proposed."

"Which only proves he has a strong sense of responsibility."

"He did." Brie's grin quickly faded. "But the absence of a huge diamond on your finger suggests that you turned him down."

"I don't think a baby—or even two babies—is a reason for two people who barely know each other to get married."

"Did you say two babies?"

Haylee nodded.

Her cousin's wife chortled. "No wonder your face went white when Caleb mentioned the idea of twins."

Rohan Sullivan, aka "Sparky," was about six-and-a-half-feet tall with frizzy red hair and a quick smile. But it wasn't only his physical appearance that distinguished him so completely from Haylee's former boss—Rohan was more than happy to add a female electrician to his crew. Or any electrician, as there was a definite shortage of qualified tradespeople willing to live and work in a small town in northern Nevada.

As he'd said during their telephone interview, "It doesn't bother me if you pee sitting down or standing up as long as you know how to use a Megger."

Haylee did and she was hired.

She started work at 8:00 a.m. and clocked out at 4:00 p.m. But living with Caleb and Brielle at the Circle G meant that she had to be out of the house shortly after seven each morning to ensure she made it to work on time. And then she got to do the forty-minute drive again at the end of the day.

She'd anticipated that living and working in Haven would make it easier to get together with Trevor, but she didn't see him at all the first week. The second week, he was out of town at a trade show for three days, but they agreed to meet at Diggers' for dinner Friday night.

Of course, having dinner in town required Haylee to make another trip back and forth to the ranch so that she could wash off the sweat from her day and make herself pretty—or at least presentable—for a date with the father of her babies. After her shower, she sat on the edge of the bed to put on her socks and closed her eyes for just a minute.

Dr. Robertson had assured her that tiredness was a common problem for many expectant moms in the first trimester. She'd also warned that many of the usual signs and symptoms might be amplified due to the fact that Haylee was carrying two babies, but that she should start to feel a little more energetic by the second semester.

She couldn't wait...

* * *

"Are you ready to order?" Deanna asked.

Trevor glanced at the time displayed on his phone. "Yeah. I'll take a southwest burger with a side of waffle fries, to go."

"Good choice," she said, collecting the two menus that had been set on the table and moving away to punch in his request at the order station.

He tried calling Haylee again, but the call went directly to voice mail. So he texted, again, but there was no response.

They'd agreed to meet at seven o'clock, and it was now almost eight. Obviously she wasn't just running a few minutes behind schedule—in which case she most likely would have called or texted him to say so—she'd stood him up.

When Deanna brought his check along with his meal packaged to go, he paid for the food and left a generous tip in the hope that she wouldn't tell all her coworkers that he'd been stood up.

He wasn't just annoyed that Haylee was a no-show, he was sincerely disappointed. And worried. If she'd changed her mind about meeting him for dinner, why didn't she let him know?

And why wasn't she answering her phone?

That was the question at the forefront of his mind when he knocked on his cousin's door.

"Trevor, this is a surprise." Brielle stepped away from the door, inviting him in.

"Is Haylee here?"

Of course, he knew that she was, because he'd parked behind her car in the driveway.

"She is, but she's upstairs. Sleeping."

"Sleeping?"

"When she came in after work, she said she was going to take a shower and then head back into town for dinner, but—oh, she was supposed to meet you," his cousin realized.

He nodded.

"I'm sorry," Bric said. "I saw her sprawled out on top of the covers, fast asleep, when I went upstairs to give Colton his bath, and I figured she'd just changed her mind about going out. If I'd realized you had plans, I would have woken her."

"I'm glad you didn't," he said. "She obviously needed sleep more than food."

"The first trimester is hard," Brie said sympathetically. "And more so, I imagine, carrying two babies."

He sighed. "She told you?"

"I don't think she really meant to," his cousin admitted. "But my pregnancy wasn't so long ago that I couldn't recognize the signs."

"Can you do me a favor?" he asked.

"Sure," she agreed readily.

"Can you check her phone and maybe plug it in? I think the battery probably died."

"I did wonder why you'd driven all the way out here instead of calling," Brie said.

"And if it's not password protected, maybe delete the twenty-seven text messages I sent?"

She bit her lip, hiding a smile. "I'll see what I can do."

Trevor said goodbye and walked out, still disappointed that he hadn't got to see Haylee but no longer worried that something had happened to her.

On his way to his truck, he crossed paths with Caleb, returning to the house.

"It'd be easier for me to pretend I didn't know you hooked up with my cousin if you didn't come sniffin' around her while she's staying here," the rancher said.

"So you know, too," Trevor realized.

"I wish I didn't. And I can't imagine—I don't want to imagine—how it happened. Haylee is hardly your usual type."

"You don't think I'm attracted to beautiful, smart, sexy women?" he challenged.

Now the other man looked thoughtful. "Not many people see Haylee that way. Of course, not many people have seen her dressed up like she was at the wedding. *I* almost didn't even recognize her."

Trevor couldn't deny that it was the dress with the short skirt that first snagged his attention. But then, when she'd looked at him, it was her eyes that had held him captive. And later, it was her smile that further entranced him. And the more time he spent with her, the more he liked her.

"Well, I'll be damned," Caleb mused, taking in his expression. "You really do have a thing for her, don't you, Blake?"

"You stay out of my business, Gilmore, and I'll stay out of yours," Trevor told him.

"Deal."

Trevor reached out to slap the snooze button on his alarm, but the damn thing wouldn't stop ringing. Because it wasn't his alarm, he finally realized, it was his phone.

He peeled open his eyes to glance at the clock as he swiped to connect the call.

"'lo?"

"I'm *so* sorry."

"Haylee?"

"Ohmygod—did I wake you?"

"It's 7:00 a.m. on a Saturday."

"I didn't realize it was so early. I woke up and saw your text message and wanted to call right away to tell you that I was sorry."

"Did you say *message* or *messages*?"

"Message," she said again.

Thank you, Brielle.

"And I am. Sorry, I mean."

"It's okay," he said. "It was my fault for making plans at the end of the week."

"Maybe we could reschedule for tonight," she suggested. "If you don't have other plans."

"I'm heading over to Crooked Creek for a few hours this afternoon, to help my grandfather bale hay, but tonight sounds good."

"Seven o'clock at Diggers'?"

"Actually, I've got a better idea."

"Are you going to tell me what it is?"

"No," he said. "But I'll pick you up at seven."

"I bet he's taking you to that fancy restaurant in the hotel," Finley said, when Haylee was Skyping with her later that afternoon.

Though she missed seeing her sister—and Simon—

every day, it seemed to Haylee as if they'd talked more in the two weeks since she'd been gone than they had when they were actually living together. She talked to her dad and Colleen, too—on Sundays and Wednesdays, because Robert Gilmore liked to have a schedule and stick to it. And he didn't like to video chat, instead calling Haylee from his landline phone on predetermined times and dates.

"Do you think so?" she asked Finley now.

"Well, he said it was a better plan than Diggers', and the only other restaurants in town are Jo's Pizza and Sunnyside Diner."

"How fancy is fancy?" Haylee wondered. "And what am I supposed to wear?"

"The dress you wore to the anniversary party would be perfect."

Maybe. *If* it still fit over the growing curve of her belly without announcing her pregnancy to the world. "Do I have to wear heels with the dress?"

"Yes, you have to wear heels with the dress," her sister confirmed. "It's an implicit part of the agreement between a man and a woman when he takes her out for a nice meal."

"You might be wrong about where we're going," Haylee pointed out. "Maybe all-day breakfast is the new dinner trend."

"I'm not wrong," Finley said. "But right now, I have to run to a major fundraiser for an up-and-coming political candidate—big names and bigger dollars."

"Have fun," Haylee said.

"Not likely," her sister said. "But we'll talk tomorrow. I want to hear all the details about dinner with the daddy of your babies."

"We'll talk tomorrow," she confirmed.

"One more thing," Finley said, before she signed off.

"What's that?"

"Wear sexy underwear, just in case."

Chapter Twelve

Finley wasn't wrong, Haylee acknowledged, as she looked around the restaurant.

Trevor had managed to wrangle an eight o'clock reservation at The Home Station, and it absolutely lived up to the "fancy" descriptor.

"This is really nice," she said.

"Wait until you try the food."

"That good?"

"The chef, Kyle Landry, studied at the School of Artisan Food in England."

"How'd he end up here?" she wondered.

"He grew up here," he told her. "In fact, his mom is Jolene Landry, of Jo's Pizza."

"For future reference, I would have been just as happy with pizza."

"There's nothing that compares to Jo's," he agreed. "But the menu here uses locally sourced ingredients to create hearty meals to satisfy the hungry rancher and impress the sophisticated traveler."

"Why does that sound as if you're reading it from somewhere?"

He turned his menu around, to show her the restaurant's mission statement on the first page.

"Which I would have seen if I'd actually opened the cover of mine," she noted, and did so now.

"Everything sounds good," she said, her gaze skimming over the offerings a second time.

"Then order one of everything," he suggested.

"I'm hungry," she acknowledged. "But I'm not *that* hungry."

"But you're eating for three," he reminded her.

"If only that were true," she said. "According to the doctor, I should only be consuming an extra three hundred calories a day in the first trimester—although I get to bump that up to almost seven hundred in the second and nine hundred in the third."

"But what are you going to have tonight?" he asked, as the server, who'd introduced herself as Erin, approached their table again.

"I think I want to start with the arugula and pear salad with Gorgonzola dressing."

"One of my favorites," Erin said.

"And then—" she looked at the menu again "—the chicken breast stuffed with spinach and mushrooms served on a bed of risotto."

Trevor made a face. "Sounds like a lot of green stuff to me."

"Green vegetables are good for you," she said.

"And for you, sir?" the server prompted.

"I'll start with the shrimp and pork wontons followed by the prime rib au jus with fingerling potatoes and baby carrots."

"Can I make a recommendation?" Erin asked.

"Of course," Trevor said.

"Save room for dessert," she said with a wink, then went to place their orders.

"I'm glad I saved room for dessert," Haylee said, as she pushed the parfait glass away.

"You liked the mousse?"

"It was white chocolate mousse with dark chocolate something-or-other garnish—what's not to like?"

"Then why did you only eat half of it?"

"Because even half was probably more than three hundred calories."

"Do you want to try my banana cake with caramel ice cream? It's amazing."

"You are the devil, aren't you?"

He grinned and nudged his plate toward her.

She retrieved her dessert spoon from the parfait glass and scooped up some of his dessert. Sliding the spoon between her lips, she closed her eyes, humming in appreciation of the rum-roasted bananas with the spongy cake and sweet ice cream.

"Yeah, that's good, too. Really good."

He liked watching her eat. She didn't pick at her meal, pretending she wasn't hungry, as other women he'd dated had sometimes done. No, Haylee ate like a person who enjoyed good food, although the sounds she made to express her enjoyment stoked in him a different kind of appetite.

She opened her eyes then and found him staring at her. "Do I have something on my face?"

She didn't wait for his answer, but lifted her napkin to her mouth.

He reached across the table to touch her arm, halting her scrubbing. "There's nothing on your face."

"Then why are you staring at me?"

"I sometimes forget how beautiful you are," he admitted. "And then I look at you and you actually take my breath away."

"Did the bartender maybe slip some rum into that glass of Coke?"

"You're a smart, capable woman who has plenty of self-confidence when it comes to your professional capabilities, but you shy away from personal compliments," he noted. "Why is that?"

"Maybe because I don't get a lot of personal compliments," she said.

"I can't be the first man who's told you that you're beautiful."

"And if I said that you were?"

"I'd say that there's something wrong with all the guys in California."

"Or maybe all the charm was taken by the guys in Nevada."

"Maybe," he agreed, as he handed his credit card to Erin to settle up their bill.

* * *

"I've been thinking about it," Trevor said, as he drove her back to the Circle G. "And I think you should move in with me."

"Whoa!" She twisted in her seat to look at him. "Where did *that* come from?"

"You've been in Haven for two weeks now, and tonight is the first chance we've had to get together."

"I came to Haven to work," she reminded him.

"I know," he admitted. "But I didn't think the job—and all the back-and-forth—was going to be such a time-suck. It's obvious that it's wearing you out."

"You work as much as I do," she pointed out.

"You're right," he acknowledged. "But you said that one of the reasons you decided to take the job in Haven was so that we'd have the opportunity to spend time together and get to know one another better."

"Which is what we were doing tonight."

"And now, we've got a half-hour drive back to the Circle G. A drive that you have to do every morning to get to work and every afternoon to get back again—but that you wouldn't have to do twice each day if you were living in town with me."

It was actually closer to a forty-minute drive, which she didn't point out to Trevor as it would only add weight to his argument. And it was true that, by the time she made the drive back to her cousin's house at the end of every day, she was usually ready to fall into bed exhausted. But of course, she didn't, because Brielle was always eager for adult company after being alone with her adorable—and undeniably demanding—infant son all day. So Haylee would hang out in the kitchen with her for a while, keeping an eye on Colton while the little guy's mom was busy getting dinner ready.

Haylee felt guilty that she was living under their roof and didn't do more, but Brielle insisted that cooking for three people was no more work than cooking for two. Plus, she told her houseguest with a wink, Finley had called ahead to warn her that Haylee was a hazard in the kitchen.

"You're not saying anything," Trevor noted, when she remained silent for a long moment.

"I'm trying to process this unexpected invitation," she admitted. "You know I don't cook, right?"

"I didn't know," he said. "But I didn't ask you to move in with me so that you could cook for me. Although now that you mention it, I'm wondering how you can claim not to cook when I've eaten your peanut butter cup cookies."

"That's baking, not cooking."

"How is it different?" he challenged. "You combine ingredients, put them in the oven for a specified amount of time, and take them out again when they're transformed into something else."

"Technically, baking is a type of cooking," she allowed. "But it's the only kind I do."

"It doesn't matter," he said. "Because I'm not asking you to cook. Or clean. I have a service that comes in every Thursday to dust and vacuum."

"What about scrub toilets?" she asked. "I hate scrubbing toilets."

"They do that, too," he assured her.

"Do you have a spare bedroom?"

"Three of them," he said. "You can take your pick—or you can share mine."

She ignored the deliberately provocative suggestion—and the "yes, please" clamoring of her hormones. "Why do you have a four-bedroom house?"

"Because the price was right and real estate is always a good investment."

"So they say," she agreed.

"What do *you* say? About moving in, I mean," he clarified.

"It would be convenient to live in town," she acknowledged. "I'm just not sure it's a good idea."

"I was joking about sharing my bedroom, if that's your concern."

"Were you?" she challenged.

"No," he admitted. "I mean, if you were interested in sharing my bed, I wouldn't say no. But if you're concerned that I'd take advantage of you staying with me to try to seduce you, I promise you that I won't."

"So we'd just be…roommates?"

"And maybe friends."

"You want to be friends?" she asked dubiously.

"It seems like a good place to start," he pointed out reasonably. "Since eventually we're going to be parents together."

She didn't know if she could be friends with him when she couldn't be around him without thinking about what had happened that night in her hotel room. When he smiled, she remembered the feel of those lips against hers. When he touched her arm, she remembered the feel of those hands caressing other parts of her body.

It wasn't just that she couldn't stop thinking about the fact that she'd been naked with him, but that her traitorous body wanted her to get naked with him again. She wanted to feel the way she'd felt when she was in his arms. Desirable. Desired.

"So…what do you say?" Trevor asked, as he pulled into the long, winding lane that led to the Circle G.

There were all kinds of reasons that she should say no. So many things that could go wrong. But when she opened her mouth to respond, she didn't express any of those concerns.

"I say 'thanks for dinner, Roomie.'"

Haylee missed her family.

Though she was enjoying her work and especially the time she was spending with Trevor, she was conscious of the five-hundred-mile distance between Haven and Oakland. Between her and her siblings and her dad and stepmom.

She FaceTimed with Finley almost every day and talked to her dad and or Colleen a couple of times a week, on a predetermined schedule. So when her phone rang at precisely 8:00 p.m. Sunday night, she couldn't help but smile as she connected the call.

"What's this I hear about you renting a room in town now?" her dad asked, after their usual exchange of pleasantries was complete.

"I'm renting a room in town now," she said.

"What was wrong with the room you had at your cousin's house at the Circle G?"

"I loved spending time with Caleb and Brielle and

Colton, but it was a forty-minute commute to and from my job."

"If the job isn't working out, then you should come home," Robert said.

"The job's working out fine," Haylee told him. "In fact, I'm really enjoying it. I just wasn't enjoying the long drive at the beginning and end of every day."

"I don't like the idea of you living alone in town. It's not safe."

"Haven's a lot safer than Oakland. Colder, too," she said, in a deliberate effort to shift the topic of their conversation.

"One of the things I definitely *don't* miss about Nevada," he said.

And she breathed a sigh of relief that the topic of her living arrangements had been abandoned—at least for the moment.

"Are there things that you do miss?" she asked him now.

"Family," he admitted. "Sometimes I forget how much until I go back for a visit and then have to say goodbye again." Then he paused, and she could picture him shrugging. "But ranching wasn't in my blood the way it is in my brothers'—I'm happier near the ocean, running my company."

He said it casually, as if Gilmore Logistics was a neighborhood shop when it was actually an international shipping conglomerate.

"But you seemed to enjoy catching up with them when you were in town for Grandma and Grandpa's anniversary party."

"Sure," he agreed. "Just because we have different

interests doesn't mean we don't get along. But speaking of people who were at the party—have you seen any more of that Blake boy who crashed it?"

"His name is Trevor, Dad. And it's not crashing if you're invited."

Of course, she hadn't actually invited Trevor, but there was reason to let her father know that.

"I'll take that as a yes," he grumbled.

"I don't understand how you can dislike him when you don't even know him."

"He's a Blake—that's all I need to know."

Haylee wanted to put her head down and bang it against the desk.

Instead, she tried logic and reason. "The land dispute between the Gilmores and Blakes happened long before you were born," she pointed out. "Don't you think it's kind of silly to be holding a grudge over something that had nothing to do with you?"

"It is what it is," he said stubbornly.

And her father being her father, she knew she wasn't going to change his mind tonight, so she steered the conversation to another topic again.

"You have to tell them," Devin said, when Trevor stopped by the following Tuesday afternoon to pick up the laptop he'd rebuilt for him.

The "them" was obviously their parents, and Trevor knew he was right, but it still wasn't a conversation he was eager to have.

"I know," he admitted. "But Haylee and I agreed to keep the news quiet until after the first trimester."

"I'm not talking about the babies—although yes, that, too."

Trevor frowned. "Then what are you talking about?"

"Haylee living with you."

"How the hell do you know that?"

"It's a small town," his brother reminded him.

"And she only moved in two days ago," he pointed out.

"So…how's it going so far?"

"Quietly," Trevor said.

"Huh?"

"We're mostly tiptoeing around one another."

"Living together is a big step," Devin said.

"I know, but it seemed…expedient," he decided.

"Expedient?" His brother laughed. "Oh, please tell me that's the word you used when you asked her to move in."

"Of course not. I'm not a complete idiot."

"That's debatable."

"So who told you?" he asked now.

"No one would ever gossip directly to me about you, but I overheard the news at The Daily Grind, The Trading Post and the library."

"The library?"

Devin shrugged. "There's a new librarian who's kind of cute. Anyway, the point is that it won't be long before the news makes its way to Miners' Pass."

"You're right," Trevor acknowledged. "I just wanted to give Haylee a chance to settle in and hopefully decide she likes me before I subject her to Lorraine and Elijah."

"Your call," his brother said. "But don't say I didn't warn you."

* * *

Their first disagreement had been about the payment of rent. Trevor didn't even want to discuss the matter, assuring her that he didn't need or want her money, but Haylee had insisted so she could honestly tell her father that she was renting a room in town in order to be closer to work.

Just another white lie, she'd assured herself, but she knew it was only a matter of time before the collective weight of all those lies brought down the house of cards she was living in.

Still, her argument at least persuaded Trevor, who agreed to accept a nominal sum—which he planned to put into a savings account for their babies. In exchange, he gave her a key and the code to the alarm system, then carried her suitcase up to the room she'd chosen.

It was the second smallest of the three guest rooms on the upper level, but she told him she liked the soft periwinkle blue color on the walls. Truthfully, she'd chosen the room because it was the farthest from his—because why tempt fate? Her hormones already rioted whenever he was in the same room with her, and she wasn't sure she'd be able to control them if there was only one thin wall between her and the father of her babies.

If Trevor experienced any residual feelings of attraction toward her, he did an admirable job of controlling them. He didn't kiss her or touch her, except inadvertently, or even flirt with her. And he certainly didn't say or do anything that suggested he laid awake in his bed at night, thinking of her just down the hall in her bed.

She was relieved, of course.

And maybe just the teensiest bit disappointed.

Living with Haylee was torture—and it was only the end of week one! How was he ever going to survive the next five weeks without losing his mind? And a lot of help he'd be to her in the second half of her pregnancy if he was in a padded room.

It shouldn't have been a big deal. Having lived with Alannis for nearly a year, he figured he knew what he was getting himself into when he suggested that Haylee move in.

He was wrong.

On the positive side, Haylee was surprisingly low maintenance. She didn't fuss with her hair or obsess about her clothes. In fact, she rarely even bothered to put on makeup. But she always smelled good, and just a whiff of her body wash in the morning was enough to have him walking around in a semi-aroused state for the rest of the day. And the way her eyes lit up when he walked in the kitchen, as if she was happy to see him, well, what man wouldn't respond to that? Not to mention her smile, which never failed to make him crave the sweet taste of that perfectly shaped mouth.

And just this morning, he'd walked into the laundry room to find her pink bra and matching panties draped over the drying rack. Which, of course, brought back vivid and erotic memories of the night he'd had the pleasure of peeling the sexy garments from her sexier body and—

"Trevor?"

He snapped back to the present. "Did you say something?"

"Just that I don't want my being here to interfere with your plans," she told him.

"What plans?" he asked, certain that he'd missed part of the conversation while he'd taken his mental detour.

But she lifted a shoulder. "How am I supposed to know? But I'm guessing that you don't usually spend every Friday and Saturday night at home."

"Not every Friday and Saturday," he acknowledged. "Although my social calendar has a lot more empty pages than most people would believe."

"I'm only saying that you shouldn't feel compelled to curtail your…usual activities just because I'm living here temporarily."

He stared at her now, torn between bafflement and amusement. "Are you talking about sex?"

She averted her gaze. "Not necessarily," she hedged. "Although I recognize that's probably part of your usual extracurricular routine, I was talking about dating or… whatever."

"And you're saying that you'd be okay with me bringing other women back here for…whatever?" he pressed.

She shrugged again as she played with a loose thread on the sleeve of her sweater. "It's your house, though the women might appreciate if you focused on them one at a time rather than as a plurality."

There had to be something wrong with him that he found himself turned on by her convoluted words and prim tone, but there was no denying that he was. Or maybe it was just that they were talking about sex, albeit in abstract terms.

"Since you brought up the subject," he said, "I feel compelled to confess that I have been focused on one woman."

"Well, then… I'll be sure to stay out of your way if you want to bring her here."

"Haylee…" He paused, waiting for her to look at him. When she finally did, he smiled. "I'm talking about you."

She swallowed. "Me?"

He nodded. "I haven't wanted anyone else since the night we spent together."

"Is it because…do you feel…responsible…for taking my virginity?"

"When I think about that night, responsible is the very least of what I feel," he assured her.

"What do you feel?"

"Answering that question might venture into dangerous territory," he warned. "So I'm just going to say that you're an amazing, intriguing and unforgettable woman."

Haylee was too guileless to heed his implicit warning, instead asking, "Then why haven't you kissed me, even once, since I've been here?"

"Because I promised you that, if you moved in here, I wouldn't try to seduce you." A promise that was increasingly testing the limits of his self-control.

"I only asked about kissing," she said, her cheeks turning pink. "Not…seduction."

"They're not so very different, when the kissing is done right," he told her. "And the next time I kiss you, you can be sure that I'll do it right."

Chapter Thirteen

Haylee was *freezing*.

An unexpected cold front had swept through the area, dropping temperatures well below seasonal norms, and she clamped her jaw tight to prevent her teeth from chattering as she stepped into the bucket. She didn't ordinarily mind working outdoors, but she was quickly realizing that she didn't have the wardrobe to work outside in twenty-degree weather.

"You going to be okay up there?" Sparky asked.

"I'll be fine," she said, as she flexed her fingers to maintain blood flow to the frigid digits.

"You need to get some Hot Mitts," he told her.

"What?"

He grinned and shook his head. "California girl."

"And proud of it. Shivering," she acknowledged. "But proud."

"Hot Mitts are activated hand warmers," he explained. "You take them out of the package, pop them inside your gloves and then they keep your hands warm all day."

"Whoever invented those is a genius," she decided. "Is there a whole body version?"

"Unfortunately not. You'll have to talk to your boyfriend about keeping the rest of you warm," he said, with a wink.

"Let's just get this job done so we can break for lunch and I can wrap my hands around a hot bowl of soup."

There were plenty of assistants scurrying around the offices of Blake Mining, any one of whom Trevor could have tapped to run paperwork over to the courthouse. But Haylee had mentioned that she was going to be working in town square this week, so he decided to make the trip himself and maybe steal her away for lunch.

After he'd finished in the clerk's office, he headed back outside. A white panel van with the familiar Sparky's Electric logo was parked on the side of the road and the man himself was pacing the sidewalk with a phone to his ear.

He finished up the call as Trevor approached and then tucked the phone into his pocket. "What's up?"

"I thought I might take Haylee to lunch, if she's around."

"She's around but she's busy," Sparky said, pointing. Trevor, following the direction indicated, nearly had a heart attack when he saw the bucket perched at least twenty-five feet in the air, and a figure in dark overalls securing lights to the peaked roof.

"That's Haylee up there?"

"Yep. She's making good progress, but I'd guess it's going to be at least an hour before she's done."

"Maybe another day then," he decided, suddenly no longer hungry.

He'd thought he understood what her job entailed. But he realized now that he'd chosen to focus on the fact that she looked sexy as hell with a tool belt slung around her hips and a hard hat on her head rather than the potential dangers she faced when she went to work every day.

Sure, there were all kinds of codes and regulations designed to keep her safe, but still, equipment could fail or malfunction, accidents could happen.

And he knew from experience, sometimes bad things happened for no reason at all.

A long hot shower helped Haylee thaw out at the end of the day. Even better, after she was dry and dressed again, she walked into the kitchen and found Trevor standing at the stove, stirring something in a pot. The sweet scent of chocolate filled the air.

She looked at the array of ingredients on the counter. "You made hot chocolate from scratch?"

"I'm more than just a pretty face, you know."

She was beginning to realize that he was so much more than she'd imagined. And the more she got to know him, the more she realized he was a man she could seriously fall for—if she was foolish enough to let herself fall.

Which, of course, she wasn't.

"Actually, it was your hot body that first caught my eye," she said lightly.

"Was it?"

"Apparently I'm shallow that way."

"And yet that hot body is here, every day, and you haven't once taken advantage of it," he noted.

"You said you wanted to be friends," she reminded him.

"I say a lot of stupid things," he said, making her laugh.

"Whipped cream or marshmallows?" he asked.

"Whipped cream," she said.

He piled a mountain of whipped cream onto the cocoa, then grated chocolate on top of the whipped cream.

"What did I do to deserve this?"

"You were stuck outside all day."

"That's the job," she reminded him, as she sat at the table and wrapped her hands around the mug.

"I know," he said. "But I didn't know that you'd be the one in the bucket twenty-five feet in the air."

"What did you think—that I just flipped the switch on a breaker when all the work was done?"

"I guess I didn't think about it enough," he admitted.

"Do you have a problem with my job?" she asked, seeming to brace for his response.

"Of course not," he denied. "I just didn't expect that I'd worry about you every morning when you walked out the door to go to your job."

"You don't have to worry," she told him. "I would never jeopardize our babies."

"I'm not worried about our babies."

"You're not?"

"No," he said. "Because I know you're taking care of them. I worry about you, because you won't let anyone take care of you. Because you won't let me take care of you."

"I don't need anyone to take care of me," she insisted. "But I appreciate that you want to. And—" she lifted her mug to her lips again "—I appreciate the hot chocolate."

Haylee sat cross-legged on top of her bed with her laptop open.

"How's my favorite guy?" she asked, trying not to think about the one down the hall who, despite all his sexy talk, still—three days later—had not kissed her.

The sound of contented purring came through her speaker, making her smile.

Of course, Simon wasn't responding to her question as much as the behind-the-ears scratch he was getting from Finley, on whose lap he was perched while Haylee and her sister Skyped.

"I think he's maybe finally starting to forgive you for ditching him to run off and live with some guy in Nevada."

"I came here to work," Haylee reminded her sister. "And Simon knows that I wanted to bring him with me."

"Does he?" Finley teased, shifting the cat so he was centered in front of the camera. "Does this look like a cat that knows—or even cares? He only cares that he's got food and water in his bowls, and a clean litter box."

Which was the reason Finley had insisted that Haylee leave her beloved feline in California with her, because she didn't want her pregnant sister to risk toxoplasmosis through exposure to soiled kitty litter.

"Well, you could tell him that I love him and miss him," Haylee said.

"I do," Finley promised. "Every day."

"I love you and miss you, too."

"Don't," her sister said firmly.

Haylee nodded, appreciating that the single word warning was intended to steer them away from a path that would end up with both of them in tears. But at least she had pregnancy hormones as an excuse for her turbulent emotions.

"How are Dad and Colleen doing?" she asked now, because she missed them, too.

"Didn't you talk to them last night?"

"Just Dad, and you know he doesn't say too much."

"Then you don't know that Colleen's niece and her husband are expecting," Finley guessed. "The baby's not due until April, but they're so excited, they couldn't resist sharing the news. I stopped by the warehouse the other day and caught Colleen shopping online for baby stuff."

Haylee sighed. "I already feel guilty enough because I haven't told them."

"So *tell them*," Finley urged.

"I will," she promised, because she knew that she had to—even if she had yet to figure out the how and when.

Thankfully, Finley didn't press for specific details, asking instead, "How are things in Haven?"

"A lot colder than I anticipated," Haylee confided.

"The temperature really dropped this week, so my Saturday is probably going to be wasted shopping for warmer—and bigger—clothes."

Her sister sighed. "Only you would think shopping is a waste of time."

"It's certainly not my idea of fun."

"Obviously I need to make another trip to Nevada."

"I need clothes for work and leisure. Not party dresses or palazzo pants and sequined tops."

"Those palazzo pants look great on you," Finley said. "But I bet you didn't even take them with you."

"There was a finite amount of space in my suitcase—and they probably wouldn't fit me right now, anyway," she grumbled. "All my clothes are starting to feel snug, and I've completely given up even trying to button my favorite jeans."

"That's because you're growing my nieces or nephews inside of you. And I promise, if even one of your babies is a girl, I'll teach her everything you don't know about fashion."

"Because you're going to be the best auntie ever."

"I will," Finley promised. "Of course, if you have a daughter who is anything like you, she might only accessorize with hard hats and tool belts."

"And my son might be a clothes horse."

"And since you're obviously not, I'll be there on Friday."

"Don't you have a big event this weekend?" Haylee asked, because her sister's weekends were always booked.

"The Forrester-Osborne wedding," Finley said. "Canceled."

"Oh, no." Haylee could imagine her sister's disappointment and frustration to have an event canceled after she'd put in so much hard work—as Finley always did—to prepare for it.

"The stress of the wedding just got to be too much for the bride and groom, so they ran off to Vegas and eloped."

"Did they really?"

Finley nodded. "The bride's parents were livid, but they paid the full tab for the five hundred–plus guests, arranged to have the flowers distributed to nearby hospitals, donated the meal to a local food kitchen and sent me a case of champagne—really good stuff.

"Plus I now have the whole weekend off," she continued. "Because there's no rehearsal dinner on Friday or wedding brunch on Sunday. And before you tell me that I can't abandon Simon, I know Colleen will be happy to watch him for a few days."

"In that case, I'll see you on Friday," Haylee said, not just because she'd be foolish to decline her sister's offer to help her shop, but because she missed her like crazy already.

"Will you be able to pick me up at the airport, or should I make other arrangements?"

"Send me your flight details when you have them, and I'll figure something out."

Finley didn't look particularly pleased when she saw Trevor waiting for her at the airport.

"I guess Haylee couldn't make it," she said.

"My schedule's more flexible than hers," he said, reaching for her bag.

"I've got it," she said, extending the handle of the wheeled carry-on to pull it behind her.

He shrugged and led the way through the double doors to the parking lot.

Finley followed, sucking in a breath as she stepped outside. "Haylee was right," she muttered. "It's cold here."

"Welcome to October in northern Nevada," he said. "Although this recent cold snap is a little colder than usual."

She didn't respond, but he suspected that Haylee's sister had clamped her teeth together to prevent them from chattering.

He opened the passenger door so that she could get out of the wind, and this time, she didn't protest when he reached for her bag to toss it onto the back seat.

He climbed behind the wheel, turned the key and cranked up the heat. Finley rubbed her hands together as he pulled out of the parking lot and headed toward Haven.

Twenty minutes later he broke the silence to say, "You were a lot chattier when I met you in Oakland."

"That was before I knew you'd knocked up my sister," she told him.

"It was a joint effort."

She didn't look amused.

"What about raising the babies—is that going to be a joint effort, too?" Finley challenged.

"Absolutely," he confirmed.

She seemed taken aback by his ready agreement.

"It would be a lot easier for both of you if you were married."

"I agree."

Finley frowned. "Well, that wasn't as hard as I expected."

"The hard part is convincing your sister," he told her.

"You've discussed this with her?"

"Tried to. She thinks that a baby—or even two babies—isn't a good enough reason to get married."

"Are you telling me that you asked her to marry you?"

He nodded. "More than once."

"Hmm."

"What does that mean?"

"I'm considering the possibility that I might have misjudged you."

"Maybe you could consider nudging your sister toward the idea of marriage," he suggested.

"Maybe I will," she said.

"Other than that, do you have any specific plans while you're in town?"

"We're going to some place called Battle Mountain to go shopping tomorrow."

"You're likely to be disappointed by the offerings in the shops compared to California," he warned.

"Haylee's only interest is in winterizing her wardrobe," Finley said. "I'm here to ensure that 'warm' doesn't look like a fashion disaster."

"Your sister always looks good."

"You're right. Her style is different than mine, but it mostly works for her. But the dress she wore to Caleb and Brielle's wedding…"

She paused then, as if to give him a moment to remember.

As if he would ever forget.

"...I picked that out. And the underwear, too."

"Thank you," he said sincerely. "And please take my credit card when you go shopping tomorrow."

"Are you suffering from baby brain already?" Finley asked, as she unclipped a pair of leggings from the hanger and handed them to her sister.

Haylee wiggled into the pants. "Why would you think that?"

"Because you're obviously distracted—you've tried on every single item of clothing that I've handed to you without question or complaint."

"That's why we're here," she reminded her sister.

"And I can see now that you weren't exaggerating about needing not just warmer but bigger clothes." Finley splayed a hand on the curve of her sister's belly. "Your babies have already grown so much."

"I'm not going to be able to hide my pregnancy for very much longer, am I?"

"Not much," Finley agreed. "So you might want to tell Dad before everyone in Haven figures it out and he hears it through the grapevine."

"They're already talking about that Gilmore girl from California moving to town and right in with Trevor Blake."

"No doubt it's all the single girls in town gossiping— or their disappointed mothers," Finley said. "Jealous that you snapped up one of the sexiest men in town."

"I haven't snapped up anyone. Trevor only suggested that I move in with him so that I don't have to commute so far to work."

"I wouldn't be so sure about that."

"Anyway—" Haylee turned around to face the mirror again "—I'm sorry if I've seemed preoccupied."

"Don't apologize—tell me what's on your mind."

Haylee sighed. "I think I'm falling in love with him."

"And why wouldn't you?" her sister said. "He's seriously hot and totally into you, and you guys are going to have the most beautiful babies."

The mention of the babies made her smile, but it didn't eliminate the worry that niggled at the back of her mind.

"And yet, for some reason, you seem to think that falling in love with him would be a problem," Finley realized.

"Of course it would. Because I don't have any experience with stuff like this, and I really don't like not having control of my emotions."

"Have you never been in love before?" her sister asked curiously, as she handed Haylee another sweater to try on.

She shook her head.

"I guess I shouldn't be surprised," Finley said. "You always were so much smarter than me."

"That's not true," Haylee protested, as she studied her reflection in the full-length mirror.

"I like the style but not the color," her sister said. "It washes you out."

She tugged the sweater over her head again and folded it before adding it to the discard pile. "So how many times have you been in love?"

"Probably not as many as I believed in the moment," Finley acknowledged.

"Then it's possible that I'm wrong—that what I'm feeling isn't love at all?" she asked hopefully.

"Anything's possible," her sister agreed. "But in this case, I'm leaning toward your feelings for Trevor being the real deal."

Haylee sighed. "I don't want my heart broken. More important, I don't want my babies' hearts broken."

"This is about Mom again, isn't it?"

"I don't know. Maybe."

"You've got to get her out of your head," Finley said. "I'm not denying that her walking out screwed us all up to some extent, but Trevor seems like a really great guy. So maybe, instead of being afraid of what might go wrong, you should consider all the things that could go right."

"He *is* a really great guy," she agreed.

"And yet you turned down his proposal," her sister noted.

"He told you about that?"

Finley nodded. "What I want to know is—why?"

"He only wants to marry me because he believes it's the right thing to do, and I want him to *want* to be with me."

Now her sister shook her head. "I think the baby hormones are messing with your brain."

"No doubt," Haylee agreed.

"Because I've seen the way the man looks at you, and I can assure you, he isn't thinking about duties or responsibilities—he's thinking of you naked."

"That's just sex, and don't guys think about sex all the time?"

"Nineteen times a day," Finley told her. "On average."

"I'm not going to ask how you know that."

"I read a lot," her sister said, answering anyway. "My point is, there's nothing wrong with building a relationship on a foundation of physical attraction."

"That ship might have sailed," Haylee said, touching a hand to her belly.

"I don't think you need to worry about that." Finley gathered up the clothes her sister was buying. "Now let's go check out the lingerie department."

Chapter Fourteen

Trevor knew it had been hard for Haylee to say good-bye to her sister when Finley left. While it was true that she had a lot of family in Haven—more than in Oakland, even—she missed her parents and her siblings.

"What do you think about making a trip to California at the end of the month?" he suggested after they'd returned home from the airport Sunday afternoon.

"Why?" she asked.

"To see your parents—and tell them that they're going to be grandparents."

"Have you told your parents?" she challenged.

"Not yet," he admitted, though he knew that he needed to do so soon. "But you're almost fifteen weeks along now, so it should be safe to share the news."

"You're right," she agreed. "I was originally thinking I'd tell my dad when I went home for Thanksgiving, but I'll be more than five months pregnant by then and, considering how my waistline is expanding already, there might not be any hiding my condition."

"We could take advantage of Nevada Day and go to California for a long weekend," he offered.

"What's Nevada Day?"

"It's celebrated on the last Friday of October each year to commemorate the state's 1864 admission to the union. The main festivities take place in Carson City, with various events through the day, including military flyovers and a parade."

"I had no idea," she said. "Do you celebrate with your family?"

"We used to go to the capital when me and Devin were kids, but not since then. Haven has its own celebration, on a smaller scale, at Prospect Park with fireworks in the evening."

"Well, I don't want you to miss out on that," she said.

"If you're going to Oakland, I'm going with you," he said.

"It's really not necessary."

"They're my babies, too."

"Are you sure?"

"Yes, I'm sure," he told her. "But I do have one question—should I borrow a bulletproof vest?"

"My dad doesn't own a shotgun," she assured him. "Although he was on the wrestling team in high school. Or maybe it was college."

"That would be a funny story to tell at our wedding," he mused. "How I was pinned to the mat by my father-in-law."

"There isn't going to be a—"

He touched a finger to her lips, silencing her in midsentence. "Don't dig your heels in," he cautioned. "It will only be harder for you to pull them out when you change your mind later."

"I'm not going to change my mind."

He just smiled. "We'll see." Then he turned his attention to the calendar app on his phone. "I've got a meeting Thursday morning, but we could leave right after that, if you can get away from work a little early, too."

"I'll email Rohan right now," she said, refusing to call her boss Sparky, as everyone else did. She reached for her phone and scrolled through her contacts. "What's the actual date?"

"Thursday's the twenty-ninth."

"Which is my stepmother's birthday," she said, suddenly remembering.

"Does that mean there'll be cake?" he asked hopefully.

She shook her head as she began tapping her screen, typing a message.

"It was your job to order the cake and that's what you're doing now?" he guessed.

She managed a smile then. "No. It's her sixtieth birthday this year."

"And you're not allowed to have cake when you're sixty?"

She sent him a look. "My dad planned a surprise trip to Hawaii to celebrate the occasion."

"So the cake will be in Hawaii?"

"What is your obsession with cake?" she wanted to know.

"I'm not obsessed," he denied. "I just happen to like cake. Especially devil's food cake with raspberry buttercream frosting."

"Nope, not obsessed at all," she said dryly.

"It's what my mom always orders from Sweet Caroline's for my birthday," he confided.

"When is your birthday?" she asked, only now realizing that she didn't have a clue.

"March fifteenth."

"Maybe our babies will be born on your birthday," she said.

"Our babies aren't due until the twenty-fifth," he reminded her.

"But less than half of all twin pregnancies go to term."

"It might be fun to share my birthday," he decided, then winked. "As long as I don't have to share my cake."

She smiled at that, then her phone chimed, indicating receipt of a text message. She swiped the screen and sighed. "And this year, Colleen's cake will be in Hawaii."

"Which means there's no point in us going to Oakland for the Nevada Day weekend," he realized.

Now she nodded.

"You want to go to Hawaii?"

She smiled at that. "Who wouldn't? But no, we're not going to crash their private holiday."

"So when are we going to share our happy news?"

"I guess it will have to wait until Thanksgiving."

"You don't ever Skype or FaceTime?"

"Not with my dad," she said. "He's technology

averse. Besides, I really think this is something that needs to be shared not just face-to-face but in person."

"Your call," he assured her.

She just hoped she hadn't already left it too late.

"You're pretty good at that," Trevor noted, watching with some surprise as Haylee whisked away the wet diaper and slid a dry one beneath Colton's bottom.

Because why wouldn't he want to spend his Friday night babysitting someone else's child in preparation for all those future Friday nights when he'd be home with his own?

But he didn't really mind. Not as long as he was with Haylee.

"I changed a lot of my brother's diapers when he was a baby," she told him. "Apparently it's one of those things—like riding a bike—that you never really forget."

"I thought Logan was only four years younger than you."

"Almost four years," she clarified. "But I was actually referring to my half brother, Sebastian, from my mom's second marriage."

"I didn't realize your mom was still alive," he admitted. "You don't ever talk about her."

She shrugged. "There's nothing to say. We don't really have much of a relationship anymore."

"Why's that?" he asked curiously.

"Because the children from her first, failed marriage don't fit into the narrative of her new, perfect life. Not that I'm bitter," she said, all too aware of the sharp edge in her tone.

"When did your parents split up?"

"The summer after Finley and I finished fifth grade."

"You and your sister were in the same grade?"

She nodded. "My birthday's in January and hers is in December."

"Busy year for your parents," he noted. "Almost as if they had twins."

"Almost," she agreed. "Anyway, for the next few years, we were shuttled back and forth between our dad's house and our mom's apartment."

"So your mom lives in California, too?"

"Not anymore. She moved to Florida with her new husband after the wedding."

"That's...far." He wasn't sure what to say. He suddenly felt...privileged? Guilty? Just for living in a town where his entire family was little more than a stone's throw away. "How often did you see her?"

"We used to go every other Easter, Thanksgiving and Christmas and for two weeks every summer."

"And now?"

Haylee shrugged. "Maybe once every couple of years."

"Do you talk?"

"Occasionally. Between the time difference and her very busy schedule of charity events and country club lunches, it's hard to set up a call. But we keep in touch via email, regularly if not frequently."

"When are you going to tell her that she's going to be a grandmother?"

She seemed startled by the question. "I hadn't given it a single thought."

"Why not?"

"I guess because she hasn't been part of my life in so long, I can't imagine her as part of our babies' lives."

"She still needs to know."

"You're right," she acknowledged. "But let me get through breaking the news to my dad first."

"Your call," he said.

"But since we're on the subject—why haven't you told your parents?"

"Because I was hoping to be able to tell them that we were getting married first."

"The babies will be coming in March whether or not there's a ring on my finger," she reminded him.

"I know," he admitted. "But the 'whether or not' gives me hope that you haven't completely ruled out the possibility."

Haylee was teaching herself to cook.

It hadn't been a conscious decision, it just kind of happened one day that she arrived home before Trevor and saw the Mmm... Meals kit in the refrigerator. He'd apparently tried the local service a few months earlier and discovered that it greatly simplified not just meal planning and preparation but grocery shopping, too. With the ingredients assembled and step-by-step instructions provided, she considered the point he'd made about cooking not being so much different from baking and decided to give it a try.

He'd seemed pleasantly surprised to arrive home a short while later and find dinner was almost ready to go on the table. Perhaps the chicken had been a little overcooked, but he'd been so sincere in his appreciation that she was encouraged to try again. Her subsequent efforts had shown some improvement, though Trevor was usually the first one home at the end of the day and already prepping the meal when she came in.

On Wednesday, though, she found him staring at the ingredients when she walked into the kitchen.

"Is something wrong?"

"I don't remember ordering lamb and lentil stew."

"So maybe they sent the wrong kit," she suggested.

"I'm not a fan of lamb—it's too chewy," he told her. "Or stew—it's too…soupy."

She laughed at that. "We could order pizza."

"That sounds like a good plan. We haven't had pizza in…wow—has it really been *three days*?"

"I'm sensing sarcasm," she noted.

"When I walked into Jo's the other night, Kendra teased that I should ask about the frequent diner rewards."

"Is there such a thing?" Haylee asked.

"Apparently not," he said. "Because when I mentioned it to Jo, she said the reward was getting to eat her pizza."

"And she's right."

"You want pepperoni and mushrooms again?"

She wrinkled her nose. "Actually, mushrooms aren't really appealing to me these days."

"You mean since Sunday?"

"I can't help it if my taste buds are out of whack."

"So what does appeal to you these days?" he asked.

"Hmm…sausage and peppers?"

"Sweet or hot?"

"Hot," she decided.

He called Jo's to place the order.

"Do you want anything else while I'm out?" he asked Haylee.

"I don't want you to go out of your way, but we're out of chocolate milk."

"You want chocolate milk with your pizza?"

"No," she immediately denied, then reconsidered. "Probably not."

He smiled, no longer surprised by her unusual food choices. "How's our ice cream supply holding up?"

"Maybe I should go to the store with you."

"Good idea."

He grabbed a basket instead of a cart, since Haylee insisted she only wanted a few things. Ten minutes later, the basket was almost full when she said, "We missed the snack food aisle."

"What do we need from there?"

"We don't *need* anything," she admitted. "But I've been craving dill pickle potato chips."

His distaste must have been revealed in his expression, because she laughed.

"I'm guessing I won't have to share them?"

"Only if you open the bag when Devin's over," he told her.

"Hmm, maybe I better grab two bags."

"You better grab them quick if you don't want our pizza to get cold."

"I'll be right back," she promised.

He added a tub of fudge brownie ice cream to the basket, using the bag of mini marshallows as an insulator between the frozen foods and fresh, then turned around and found himself face-to-face with Lorraine Blake.

"Hello, Mother." He was more than a little surprised to run into her here because he knew that Greta—his parents' cook—was responsible for the weekly shopping. He also knew that Wednesday was the cook's day off. "What brings you here in the middle of the week?"

"We're having friends over for drinks later and your father wanted some charcuterie," she said.

He had to fight back a smile, thinking about how Haylee had responded to his use of the word "hence" and wondering how she'd react to his mother's mention of "charcuterie" in casual conversation when most people would say cold meats and cheeses.

"That's an unusual assortment of items," she noted, looking at the contents of his basket. "Even if you were a ten-year-old."

He shrugged, unaffected by her disapproval.

Of course, he had thirty-one years of experience to condition him to her exceedingly high standards and demanding nature. Nothing less than one hundred and ten percent was ever good enough for his mother, and even then, that effort had better be reflected in the results.

But Haylee didn't have that experience, and though he was sure she had to be wondering why he hadn't yet introduced the future mother of his children to his own parents, she hadn't pressed him to do so. Maybe Brielle had given her a heads-up that his parents—much like his cousin's—were too busy making money to concern themselves with supportive familial relationships.

Even so, he should have warned Haylee. He should have said something to prepare her for this moment—

and probably better prepared himself, too. Instead, she was happily oblivious as she made her way down the frozen food aisle toward him, a lamb to the slaughter.

"I found them," she said, holding the bags of dill pickle chips together over her head as if she was hoisting a trophy.

He couldn't help but smile at her enthusiasm as he waved her over.

"And who is this?" Lorraine demanded to know.

If his mother's tone had been cool before, it was downright frigid now, and her gaze—as it raked over Haylee, from the purple Converse high-tops on her feet to the denim that hugged her legs and tunic-style sweater that didn't completely conceal the swell of her fifteen-and-a-half-weeks baby bump—was icy.

His mother was, of course, dressed in a designer suit and high heels and somehow managed to look fresh after ten hours at the office.

Haylee's smile slipped and she hugged the chips against her.

"This is Haylee." Trevor slid a supportive arm across her shoulders. "Haylee, this is my mom, Lorraine Blake."

"Oh." Perhaps sensing it might be bitten off, Haylee didn't offer her hand. Instead, she nodded. "It's nice to meet you, Mrs. Blake."

"I'm sure it is," she responded.

"Is Dad here with you?" Trevor asked, attempting to deflect her attention.

"That would be convenient, wouldn't it? Then you could introduce us both to your…friend…in the middle of the grocery store."

"I'll take that as a no," he said.

"He was on a call with China when I left the office," Lorraine finally responded to his original question. "But I'm sure he'll be disappointed to know that he missed…this."

"No doubt," Trevor agreed.

"But I'm glad I ran into you," she continued, as if she didn't have the opportunity to see him every day at the office. "I've been meaning to invite you—" her gaze slid over to Haylee again "—both of you—to dinner Saturday night."

"For Devin's birthday," he guessed. He'd anticipated that there would be a family meal to celebrate the occasion, because there always was, but he hadn't decided whether or not he should subject Haylee to the event.

His mother nodded. "I do hope you can make it."

When Trevor didn't immediately respond, Haylee made the decision for both of them.

"We wouldn't miss it," she said.

Because she had no idea what she was getting herself into.

Chapter Fifteen

"Why didn't you say something?" Haylee asked, pausing in the act of applying gloss to her lips. "When your mother said we were invited for dinner—why didn't you say something?"

"Because I was trying to come up with a believable excuse as to why we couldn't make it."

She recapped the gloss and dropped it into her purse. "And how was I supposed to know that?"

"Maybe because I wasn't saying anything."

"I'm not good with silence," she admitted.

"I know," he said, teasing to lighten the mood. "I live with you."

She adjusted the skirt of her purple dress, then turned to look at her profile in the mirror. "This isn't so bad," she decided. "I look chubby more than pregnant, don't you think?"

"I think you look gorgeous," he said. "And just a little bit scared."

"Your mom is…intimidating."

"You've had three days to come up with an excuse to get out of it, if you don't want to go," Trevor pointed out.

"And I considered several," she confided. "But backing out at the last minute would be rude, and your mother already doesn't like me."

"That's not true," he denied.

"Please—we both know she wasn't happy to meet me when we ran into her at The Trading Post."

"That was my fault," he said. "I should have told her that I'd asked you to move in."

"And that I'm pregnant."

"Let's save that revelation for another day," he suggested.

"I don't see how that's possible when your mother already knows."

"Why would you think that?"

"Her disapproving tone combined with the way her gaze kept dropping to my midsection."

"That's my mother's usual tone. And she was probably focused on the potato chips. She doesn't approve of junk food."

"She doesn't approve of *me*."

"Even if that's true now, her opinion will change when she learns that you're carrying her first *and* second grandchild."

"Do you really think so?" she asked dubiously.

"Hope springs eternal," he said, though truthfully,

he'd learned a long time ago to temper his expectations whenever his parents were involved.

She picked up a square box wrapped in brightly colored paper and topped with a red bow.

"What's in the package?" he asked.

"Your brother's birthday present."

"You didn't have to get him anything."

"I wanted to," she said. "What are you giving him?"

"A six-month subscription to Mmm… Meals."

"That's the meal kit delivery service you use, isn't it?"

He nodded. "It was a gift from Devin for my birthday."

"You're kidding."

Now he shook his head.

"Bet he likes my gift better," she said.

"What is it?"

She smiled. "You'll have to wait and see."

"Relax," Trevor said, as he walked beside Haylee toward the front door of his parents' house. "You look like you're getting ready to face a firing squad."

"Maybe because that's how I feel," she told him.

"You like my brother," he pointed out.

"Are you suggesting that if I like your brother, I'll like your parents?"

"No," he said. "I'm just reminding you that you like my brother—and he adores you."

And the fact that it was Devin's birthday was the only reason that Haylee was there.

As they stepped up to the door, her hands tightened around the gift she carried. She already sensed that

Trevor's mom didn't approve of her, and she didn't hold out much hope that she'd make a better impression on his father. But she'd made an effort, dressing for the occasion in a plum-colored wrap-style dress that she'd bought on her recent shopping trip with Finley.

Trevor looked as handsome as always, casually attired in dark jeans and heather-gray fisherman knit sweater.

A uniformed housekeeper met them at the door to hang their coats and then escort them to the parlor where Mr. and Mrs. Blake were having predinner cocktails.

Haylee tried not to gawk as she walked alongside Trevor to the designated sitting room at the front of the house.

Trevor briefly made the introductions, and Lorraine was gracious enough to pretend that they were meeting for the first time. Drinks were poured—a beer for Trevor and sparkling water for Haylee—and conversation flowed, albeit not very smoothly.

"While we're waiting for your brother, why don't you help me choose a bottle of wine for dinner?" Lorraine suggested to her elder son.

"You know a lot more about wine than I do," Trevor said.

"I'm not sure that's true," she said, linking her arm through his so that he had no choice but to follow her out of the room, leaving Haylee alone with Elijah Blake.

She sipped her water and searched for something to say, finally settling on, "Your house is lovely."

"Have you been given a tour?" Trevor's dad asked.

"Just between the foyer and here."

"Come on," he said. "I'll show you around."

Haylee couldn't deny that she was curious about the house, so she fell into step beside him. He might have been in the business of mining, but he knew a lot about architecture and regaled her with details about the construction and various features of the home.

"And this is the library," Elijah said, opening a set of classic French doors into a gorgeously appointed room with a trio of arched windows and built-in floor-to-ceiling bookcases.

"It's beautiful." She ventured farther into the room, pausing when she spotted the single book on display on the middle shelf of one of the enclosed cases. The dust jacket was faded and slightly worn around the edges, but in good condition otherwise.

"Is that a first edition of *The Hobbit*?" she asked.

"It is," he confirmed.

"That was one of my all-time favorite books when I was growing up. I didn't enjoy *Lord of the Rings* as much, but I was probably just too young to appreciate it. That and the Ringwraiths gave me nightmares."

"It took me a while to track down that copy," Elijah said. "And it cost me forty thousand dollars at auction when I did."

"Wow." She appreciated literature and understood that original printings were works of art as much as books, but she was still taken aback to learn the value of it.

"Outbid a Rockefeller and an unidentified billionaire hedge fund manager from New York," he said proudly. "And when I brought it home, I couldn't imagine ever parting with it."

"I wouldn't want to give it up, either, if it was mine," she said.

"And it could be."

"Excuse me?" she said, taken aback by his suggestion.

"It wouldn't take up much room in your suitcase when you pack to go back to California," Elijah said.

"No, it wouldn't," she agreed, starting to get an idea of where the conversation was going—and desperately hoping he'd prove her wrong.

"Or I could write you a check, if you prefer."

Nope, not wrong.

"You want me to leave," she realized, feeling sick inside.

"Not just pretty but quick," he said approvingly, as he opened the top drawer of the glossy antique desk to retrieve his checkbook. "So how much do you want? What's your magic number?"

Because in his world, everything was for sale.

Everyone had a price.

"If and when I decide to go back to California, it will be because it's what Trevor and I decide," she said. "Not because you paid me."

"Trevor isn't thinking straight right now," his father argued. "He's trying to do the right thing, because that's the kind of man he is, but I'm not going to let him be taken advantage of by another girl who got knocked up—especially one named Gilmore."

So much for Trevor's theory that his mom hadn't been looking at Haylee's midsection—and her hope that the age-old feud wouldn't be a factor in her relationship with Trevor.

She took a deep breath and forced herself to count to three inside her head before she responded. "I'm going to overlook your insulting assumptions about me because you don't know me," she said, when she could finally speak calmly. "I'm even going to give you credit for looking out for your son because I haven't yet held my babies in my arms and already there isn't anything I wouldn't do for them. But I can't understand your willingness to push those babies—your grandchildren—out of your life."

"Bab*ies*?"

She nodded. "Trevor and I are having twins."

Though Elijah was apparently surprised by that revelation, he recovered quickly. "Just because you claim they're my son's babies doesn't make it true."

"It's not a claim, it's a fact," Trevor said from the doorway.

Though his tone was level, there was no mistaking the fury simmering beneath the surface.

His father dropped the checkbook back into the drawer and hastily shoved it closed. "Trevor. Son—"

"Unless the next words out of your mouth are a sincere apology to Haylee, I don't want to hear them."

"I think you've misunder—"

"Nope," Trevor said, cutting him off. "Not an apology. And not a misunderstanding, either." He shoved the bottle of wine in his hand toward his mother, who was standing beside him, then strode across the floor to grab Haylee's hand. "Let's go."

Though her stomach growled in protest of the fact that they were leaving before dinner, she didn't say anything as she slid her feet into her boots.

Devin walked through the front door as Trevor was helping with her coat. "Where are you going?" he asked, oblivious to the drama that had played out before his arrival. "You didn't eat without me, did you?"

"We're not hungry," Trevor said, at the same time Haylee's stomach growled again.

Devin's brows lifted.

"We'll pick up something from Diggers' on the way home," Trevor promised her.

She nodded, then to his brother said, "I'm sorry."

"I don't know what happened," Devin told her. "But I'm willing to bet you didn't do anything wrong."

"How much money are you willing to pony up?" she wondered, and immediately wished she could take back the question.

"So that's the direction he went," Devin realized, shaking his head and sending a worried glance toward his brother. "Now I have to say that *I'm* sorry—and promise that I'll bring you a piece of cake later." Then he winked. "If there is any leftover cake."

She smiled at that and kissed his cheek. "Your gift is on the sideboard in the parlor. Happy birthday."

Trevor had never been more furious with his parents. He wouldn't have been surprised if they'd expressed disappointment because "whoops! I did it again." But he'd never anticipated that they'd attempt to interfere in such a bold and insulting manner.

Haylee had called Diggers' to place their order while he drove, not able to get away from his parents' house fast enough. Now they were parked behind the restaurant to wait the requisite "twenty to twenty-five minutes" until their food was ready.

He didn't know what to say to Haylee, how to apologize. She had to be feeling hurt and angry, and because he'd taken her to Miners' Pass, he couldn't help but feel complicit in her emotions.

After several moments of silence, she reached over the console and touched a hand to his arm. "Are you okay?"

He turned his head to stare at her, baffled. "You're worried about *me*?"

"You're obviously upset."

"I'm seriously pissed," he said, his tone clipped.

"Okay," she agreed cautiously.

"And more sorry than you can imagine," he added, in a quieter voice.

"I was grateful for your spirited defense, but I don't blame your parents for looking out for you. And of course they'd be skeptical about paternity. You haven't asked for a DNA test, and you haven't told them that I was a virgin when we slept together."

"Because that's none of anyone's business but ours," he told her.

"And I appreciate your discretion, but they don't know me and, from their perspective—from any perspective," she acknowledged, "our relationship is moving pretty fast."

"You're right that they don't know you. But instead of trying to get to know you, my father tried to buy you off."

Haylee nodded, unable to deny that fact.

And he continued to seethe for several more minutes before she spoke again, saying, "Can I ask…about your fiancée?"

Trevor blew out a breath. "Of course he told you about Alannis."

"He only mentioned that you'd found yourself in a similar situation before," she said. "But I heard about your engagement—and the baby—from Brie."

"Then what more do you need to know?" he asked.

"For starters, why you didn't tell me."

"Because it's ancient history."

"Five years is hardly ancient history."

He shrugged. "Well, it feels like it."

He thought—*hoped*—that would put an end to the topic of his ex-girlfriend, but Haylee's next question proved him wrong.

"Were you and Alannis together for a long time?"

"A couple of years."

"I'm guessing your parents got to know her pretty well during that time."

"Not really," he said. "Regular Sunday night dinners aren't really a thing with Lorraine and Elijah—unless someone's birthday happens to fall on a Sunday. So if you're worried that they're comparing you to Alannis—don't."

"Because they didn't like her, either?" she guessed.

"They thought she got pregnant on purpose because she wanted the Blake name and money." And to this day, he couldn't be sure they were wrong. "But they agreed that getting married was the right thing to do, under the circumstances."

"Because even if she was a gold-digger at least she wasn't a Gilmore?"

"The feud has nothing to do with us," he insisted.

"If only that were true."

"Here's an idea—if we have a boy, we'll name him Gilmore, then he'll be Gilmore Blake."

"Or both the babies could have Gilmore-Blake as their hyphenated surname," she suggested.

She could see he wasn't thrilled by that suggestion, because she followed it up by saying, "But we've still got time to figure out those details."

"Yeah, I guess we shouldn't get too far ahead of ourselves," he agreed.

"I'm sorry…about the baby you lost," she said gently.

It was the first time in a very long time that anyone had mentioned the child he'd never known. The pain had faded…even the dull ache was mostly gone now. Maybe that's why he was able to confide to Haylee something he'd never told anyone else before.

"The truth is… I'm not even one hundred percent sure it was my baby."

She considered this revelation for a minute before responding, "But that didn't matter to you…did it?"

"No," he said. "It didn't matter."

His feelings for Alannis might have changed when he suspected she'd been unfaithful, but his love for the baby they were going to have together had been unwavering. The fact that Haylee had realized that, possibly before even he did, proved she was more attuned to his feelings than he'd given her credit for. "I've noticed that you catch yourself sometimes, when you start to talk about a future event with the babies—almost as if you're afraid to make plans."

"Alannis was still in her first trimester when she

lost the baby," he told her. "But we'd already ordered a crib and change table and all the other paraphernalia a baby needs."

"You were excited about being a dad."

And devastated when that dream didn't come to fruition.

But maybe a little relieved, too. Because as much as he'd been determined to be a good husband and an even better daddy, he knew that a baby wouldn't magically fix the problems that had become apparent in his relationship with Alannis in the months before her pregnancy.

"I *am* excited about being a dad," he said now, because it was true. "And I'm really glad I'm having these babies with you."

Then he leaned across the console and lightly touched his mouth to hers.

"I have to admit, I'm not really disappointed to be sitting on the sofa in your living room watching a game on TV and eating burgers and fries from Diggers'. Those ladderback chairs I saw in your parents' dining room didn't look all that comfortable. Plus I overheard your mom say something to you about osso buco—" She shuddered.

"This is much better," he agreed, grateful that she was looking on the bright side of their change of plans. "But I thought we might watch a movie instead of a game tonight."

"A movie sounds good," she agreed, lifting her cheeseburger to her mouth as he pressed a button on the remote.

Her attention was snagged by the first few bars of music even before the names Billy Crystal and Meg Ryan popped up on the screen.

"Really? This is what you want to watch?" But she was smiling now, too, pleased not just with his choice but that he'd remembered.

He shrugged. "You said it was your favorite."

"Maybe I should have warned you that it's a chick flick."

"I figured as much," he admitted.

Her gaze narrowed speculatively. "Is this a trap? We're going to watch this and then you're going to make me watch your favorite movie, and it's going to be some awful slasher film?"

He propped his feet up on the coffee table. "I don't have a favorite movie."

"Really?" She popped the tab on her soda can and sipped. "There isn't any one movie that you've seen multiple times but still can't resist watching again when you're scrolling through the channel guide and see it's on TV?"

He thought about it for a minute. "I usually can't resist the *Star Wars* movies. Except Episode One—I can skip that one."

"I liked Episode One when I first saw it," she said. "Until I realized that little Anakin Skywalker grows up to become Darth Vader."

"You don't know the power of the dark side."

She rolled her eyes. "Shut up and watch the movie."

He shut up and watched the movie.

But during the scene in the bookstore, he leaned

closer, squinting at the image on the screen. "Why does Sally's friend look familiar?"

"I should have guessed that you'd recognize her," she noted.

"But from what?"

"Picture her with side buns," she said, referencing Carrie Fisher's iconic hairstyle in the first *Star Wars* movie.

"It's Princess Leia," he realized.

She nodded.

"I have to confess, when I think of Princess Leia, I don't think about her hairstyle in Episode Four but the gold bikini in Episode Six."

"Of course you do," she noted dryly.

He just grinned.

She didn't know if he grinned when the deli scene played out, because she didn't dare look in his direction. But when the director's mother spoke what was undoubtedly the movie's most famous line, he chuckled.

Haylee kept her gaze on the screen.

The final credits had just started to roll when the doorbell rang. "I'll get it," Trevor said, gathering up the empty food and beverage containers on his way to the door—and returning with his brother.

Haylee's smile widened when she saw the plate in Devin's hand. "Is that leftover cake?"

"It is," the birthday boy confirmed, setting it on the table.

"Thanks," she said.

"No, thank *you*."

She smiled again. "I take it you liked your gift?"

"Best birthday present ever," he told her.

"I knew you'd appreciate a gift certificate for Mmm… Meals," Trevor chimed in.

"I do," Devin agreed, winking at Haylee. "But I was referring to Haylee's gift—and wondering how she managed to get her hands on a baseball signed by Mark Nickel."

"So that's what was in the box," Trevor said, because of course they hadn't been there to see his brother open it.

"I know people who know people," she said.

"And her sister Finley dated Mark when he played for the A's," Trevor said, explaining the cryptic remark to his brother.

"Did you ever get to see him play?" Devin asked.

"A few times."

"Me and Trev were at the game, three years ago, when he completed a natural cycle."

"Me and Fin were at that game, too," Haylee said.

"No kidding," Devin mused. "Just think, the two of you might have met at the coliseum three years ago."

"Somehow, in a crowd of fifty thousand–plus people," Trevor noted dryly.

"Why not? Out of all the guests at the wedding, Haylee's the one who caught your eye. An admittedly smaller gathering," Devin said. "But still, I've never seen you so quickly and completely smitten."

"Smitten?" she echoed, amused.

"Why do you think he bought those tickets to the baseball game?"

"Because the two of you were planning to go, but then you had to go out of town for business."

"You actually bought that story?"

She looked at Trevor quizzically. "It's not true?"

"It's true," he insisted. "Devin was in Montreal that weekend."

"Which you knew when you bought the tickets," his brother pointed out.

"I'll get plates for the cake," Trevor said.

Devin chuckled at his brother's hasty escape.

"Is it true?" Haylee asked, after the cake had been eaten and Devin was gone.

"Is what true?"

"Did you come to Oakland to see me?"

"Yeah," he reluctantly admitted.

"But that was before you even had a reason to suspect I might be pregnant," she realized.

He nodded.

"But…why?"

He shrugged. "Because I couldn't stop thinking about you."

"Maybe you really were smitten," she mused.

"And I'm becoming more and more each day," he told her.

She wasn't entirely sure he wasn't just teasing her, but it was something to think about.

Chapter Sixteen

"You better not be calling to say that you can't make it home for Thanksgiving," Colleen said, when she answered the phone on the Tuesday before the holiday.

"Of course I'm coming home," Haylee assured her. "I'm only calling to let you know that I'm not coming alone."

"You're bringing a guest to dinner?"

"If that's okay."

"Of course it's okay. I'm just…surprised," her stepmother said. "Is it anyone I know?"

"You met him at the anniversary party," she confided.

"The one everyone was whispering about crashing the party?" Colleen guessed.

"That's him," Haylee confirmed. "Trevor Blake."

"He seemed like a nice man—and handsome," Colleen acknowledged. "Though your father might have mumbled something about 'lying, scheming Blakes.'"

Which wasn't really a surprise, in light of the comments he'd made on the phone to Haylee, and confirmed that the Blakes weren't the only ones still holding onto a grudge.

"You've known him a while then?" her stepmother guessed.

"Yeah." Haylee glanced down at the swell of her belly.

About five months, in fact.

But, of course, she kept that to herself.

"How long have you been dating?"

If she told Colleen that they were just friends and then she showed up pregnant, her stepmother would have a million questions about the identity of the baby's father. But was it accurate to describe their relationship as dating? Or maybe accuracy wasn't as important right now as setting the stage for the big reveal.

"We've been together for a while," she acknowledged.

"And you want to introduce him to your family." Her stepmother sounded delighted at the prospect of meeting Haylee's new boyfriend.

Her first boyfriend.

"Maybe it is too soon," she decided.

"No, it's not," Colleen denied. "We'd be happy to have him join us for Thanksgiving."

"Will you promise not to give him the third degree?" she asked hopefully.

"I will, but I don't pretend to have any control over your father," her stepmother warned.

"Do you think he'll play nice if I bake a pecan pie for him?"

"I have no doubt that it will go a long way toward softening his disposition," Colleen said.

"Something smells good," Trevor noted, as he walked into the kitchen.

"Pecan pie." Haylee set the baking tray on top of the stove and closed the oven door before turning to face him.

They'd been living together for almost four weeks now, and he still made her heart pound whenever he walked into the room.

"For dessert?" he asked hopefully.

She shook her head. "For Thanksgiving."

"Because you're sucking up to your father because you haven't yet told him that he's going to be a grandfather in less than four months."

"Okay, maybe I am struggling a little to come up with the right words," she acknowledged.

"Maybe you shouldn't worry so much about the right words and just tell him. On the other hand, maybe you shouldn't say anything at all."

She stared at him incredulously. "You think I should wait until a later date to share the news? Like maybe after the babies are born?"

He chuckled. "No, I'm suggesting that your dad might realize you're pregnant when he sees you."

Now she looked down at the front of her sweater, already stretched over the swell of her belly and sighed. "I'm not going to be able to hide it much longer, am I?"

"Honey, you only think you're hiding it now."

"If I wear a bulky sweater, no one will notice."

"Maybe," he said, though his tone was dubious. "But it would have to be a really bulky sweater."

"And I'll carry the pie in front of me."

"Because that was such an effective strategy with the chips," he remarked dryly.

She sighed again. "I waited too long, didn't I? Now Thanksgiving is going to be a disaster."

"Look on the bright side."

"What's that?"

"It will have blown over by Christmas."

"I can only hope," she said.

"But since you've still got that line between your brows that you always get when you're worried about something, why don't you tell me what it is."

"I don't want our babies to be pulled in different directions at every holiday. Easter with Mom, Thanksgiving with Dad, Christmas with Mom. Then the reverse order the following year."

He tiptoed carefully, aware that he was inching onto treacherous ground. "If you married me, there wouldn't be any question about where our kids would spend Christmas, because they'd be with both of us."

"For how long?" she challenged. "How long do you think it would take until you realized it was a mistake to marry a woman you don't love?"

He tipped her chin up, forcing her to meet his gaze. "I promise you, when we get married, I will do everything in my power to make our marriage work."

"Don't you mean, *if* we get married?"

"I'm trying to think positive." He took her hand and guided her over to a chair. "And I'm positive that there's something more going on here that you're not telling me. This part I'm less sure about, but I'm guessing it has something to do with your mother."

"Why would you say that?" she asked, sinking into the seat.

He sat down beside her. "Because you don't talk about her. You happily volunteer information about your dad and stepmom, but aside from telling me that your mom's remarried and lives in Florida, you haven't told me anything about her."

"Maybe because I'm ashamed of what she did…and worried that I might turn out to be just like her."

"What did she do that was so terrible?" he asked.

"She walked out and never came back. I don't mean that we never saw her again," she clarified, though he already knew that she and her siblings had been shuffled from one home to another for some time after the separation. "But our family was never the same after that.

"She claimed that she left us with our dad because it would be less disruptive for us to stay in the house we'd always lived in. And maybe she was right, but at the time…how could we not feel as if we'd been abandoned?"

"I can't imagine what that must have been like," he admitted. He had his own issues with his parents, but at least they'd always been there.

"My dad was as confused as we were," she continued. "He had no idea there was anything wrong before she announced that she didn't want to be married anymore."

"Was there someone else?"

Haylee shook her head. "No. Not then. She said it wasn't that she didn't want to be married to my dad, but that she was taking a stand against the institution in general. That marriage was designed to oppress women, making them responsible for cooking and cleaning and raising the kids."

"I'm sorry," he said sincerely.

"My grandmother came to stay with us for a while, until my dad figured out a more long-term arrangement. Meanwhile, my mom was living in an apartment that he was paying for. But only until she could support herself, or so she claimed."

Which was probably why Haylee was so determined to earn her own income, to not be dependent on her family or—God forbid—a husband for financial support.

"She didn't have a college degree or a lot of work experience, but she eventually got a job as a hostess at the new Black & Blue Steakhouse when it opened up in town."

He recognized the name of the high-end restaurant chain and had, in fact, dined at a Black & Blue on his last trip to Vegas.

"Three years later, Dalton Burke walked into the restaurant."

"Of Burke Food Group?" he guessed, naming the company that owned and operated Black & Blue as well as a few other national restaurant chains.

She nodded again. "And suddenly marriage wasn't a

trap but a celebration. Or maybe it was an opportunity for her to get out of Oakland.

"She always had dreams of traveling the world and resented that my dad wouldn't take her all the places she wanted to go, because he doesn't like to be away from his shipping business for too long. In fact, the trip he took to Hawaii for Colleen's birthday is the first real vacation he's probably had in five years.

"Dalton's business is different. He's constantly on planes, crisscrossing the country to check on various interests here and there, or—when he's not working—jetting off to ski in Switzerland or sail the Mediterranean, and my mom's happy to go with him. Of course, they have a tutor for Sebastian, because why would he waste his time in a classroom when he could celebrate his tenth birthday at the original Legoland in Denmark?"

"That's the age you were when they separated," he remembered.

She nodded. "Coincidentally, that was the same year I learned that Santa wasn't any more real than wedded bliss."

"A tough age to have your family—and childhood illusions—fall apart," he noted sympathetically.

"Is there ever a good age?" she wondered aloud.

"Probably not," he acknowledged. "But just because your parents' marriage didn't work isn't reason to diss the whole institution."

"How about the fact that forty-five percent of all marriages end in divorce?" she said.

"I think that's a flawed statistic. And in any event, marriage shouldn't be about statistics but about sharing your life with someone you care about."

"What about love?" she challenged.

"Love?" He didn't quite manage to mask the derision in his tone.

"'To love, honor and cherish' is a keystone of the traditional vows," she pointed out.

"So we'll exchange nontraditional vows," he suggested. "Because I can promise to be a faithful husband and attentive father, but there's no way I'm ever going to fall in love with you."

His words only confirmed what Haylee already knew, but that knowledge failed to lessen the sting of his assertion.

"Thank you for that unique offer," she said coolly. "But I'm going to have to decline."

"Be reasonable, Haylee."

"This is me being reasonable," she told him, pleased that she'd managed to tamp down on her instinctive— and admittedly less rational—response, which was to tell him that there was *no way in hell* she'd ever say "yes" to such an insulting proposal.

Well, he'd blown that in spectacular fashion, Trevor realized, as he watched her storm out of the room.

Two steps forward, three steps back.

Over the past few weeks, they'd made real progress in their relationship. During that time, he'd been surprised to discover how much he enjoyed being with her. She was easy to talk to, not only knowledgeable on a wide variety of subjects but interested in learning more. She had strong beliefs and opinions, but she wasn't at all close-minded.

Except, perhaps, on the matter of marriage—that

was the one topic of discussion about which they continued to butt heads.

Half an hour later, he knocked on her open bedroom door.

"I made dinner," he said, peeking around the portal. "Are you going to come down to eat? Or do you want me to bring you a plate?"

She looked up from the book she was reading. "What's for dinner?"

"Baked chicken, scalloped potatoes and steamed broccoli."

After a brief hesitation, Haylee slid her bookmark between the pages and closed the cover. "I'll come down."

"Are you still mad?" he asked, when she ventured into the kitchen as he was dishing up the food.

"I was never mad." But she didn't look at him as he set a plate in front of her.

He wanted to take her at her word and let the matter drop, but something in her tone warned that she was hurting, and the last thing he'd ever wanted to do was hurt her. So instead he said, "You sounded mad."

She stabbed her fork into a broccoli spear. "Pregnancy hormones are running rampant in my body. You shouldn't pay too much attention to how I sound."

"I'd like to apologize anyway."

Finally she lifted her gaze to his. "What exactly are you apologizing for?"

"For letting you think that my inability to fall in love with you has anything to do with you when the truth is, I'm never going to fall in love with anyone. Ever."

She picked up her knife and sliced into the chicken. "Don't you mean 'ever again'?"

"You think I'm still heartbroken over Alannis," he realized.

"Aren't you?"

"No." He pushed his potatoes around on his plate. "But sometimes I wonder if something inside me died when the baby did. I don't mean to sound melodramatic, but it's true. Afterward, I went on with my life, but... I was mostly just going through the motions."

"I know something about that," she told him.

"Because you lost your family, too, when your mom walked out."

She nodded.

"So maybe this is a second chance for both of us," he said. "But you have to be willing to give us a chance."

"I'm here, aren't I?"

He wasn't sure if she was referring to her presence in Haven or, more specifically, at the dinner table.

Either way, he had to figure it was a step in the right direction.

"There's my pecan pie," Robert Gilmore said, when he opened the door to greet his guests—or maybe just Haylee, who stood on the porch with the promised treat in hand.

"And pumpkin," she said, referring to the pie that Trevor, standing slightly behind her, was carrying.

"Well, let pumpkin come in," Colleen said, winking at Trevor as she opened the door wider to allow them entry.

"You remember Trevor?" she asked.

"Sure," her dad said. "The party crasher."

"Rob," his wife chided.

"Yeah, yeah. Best behavior," he remembered.

Trevor grinned, unoffended. "It's nice to see you both again."

"Finley's not here yet?" Haylee asked, wondering how they'd manage to arrive before her sister, who only had to walk across the yard.

"Logan's car's in the shop, so she went to pick him up."

Which was nice of her sister but undermined Haylee's hope that their father would be less likely to blow a gasket in front of the whole family.

"Take off your coats and stay awhile," Colleen urged. "I'm just going to take these pies to the kitchen. Robert, why don't you get the kids something to drink?"

"What do you like, Blake? Beer? Wine? Whiskey?"

"A beer would be good," he said. "Thanks."

"Haylee? We've got a bottle of that Riesling you like."

"Actually, just water for me, thanks." She lowered herself onto the edge of the sofa. Trevor sat beside her and took her hand, giving it a gentle squeeze for moral support.

Her dad started out of the room, then abruptly turned around again. "Before I forget, Henry stopped by the warehouse the other day. He said business is starting to pick up again and he'll for sure have work for you early in the new year."

"Did he?" Haylee wasn't sure what else to say.

"I thought you'd be a more excited about the news— about coming home."

"It is good news," she said, as Colleen returned from

the kitchen. "It's just that Trevor and I have some news to share, too."

Her father took a few steps closer, the promised drinks forgotten. "What kind of news?" he demanded.

"I'm—"

"*We're*," Trevor interjected.

"—pregnant."

There was a moment of complete and stunned silence, followed by Colleen exclaiming, "Oh, that's wonderful news!" Then she turned to her husband, to prompt him. "Isn't it wonderful, Rob?"

The lack of an immediate reply told Haylee that he wasn't nearly as thrilled as his wife. And when he finally did respond, he was looking at Trevor.

"I wouldn't expect a Blake to know what's the right thing," he said, "so I'll tell you—it's marrying the girl you got pregnant."

"Dad—"

He silenced his daughter with a sharp glance, then shifted his attention back to her future groom.

Trevor wasn't easily intimidated, but the intensity of the older man's stare caused a bead of sweat to slowly snake down his spine. Still, he felt compelled to say, "Haylee hasn't decided if that's what she wants."

Robert's eyebrows drew together over his narrowed gaze. "*Haylee* hasn't decided?" he echoed, before turning to her again.

She lifted her chin. "Yes, Dad. It's the twenty-first century and a woman actually does get a say in such matters."

"A woman who doesn't say 'no' when a man invites

her to his bed shouldn't say 'no' when he wants to do the right thing," her father insisted stubbornly.

"Maybe we could table this discussion for another time?" Colleen suggested, starting toward the door in response to the ring of the bell.

"This discussion has waited long enough already," Robert argued.

His wife gave the expectant parents a sympathetic glance as she went to answer the summons.

"How far along are you?" the Gilmore patriarch asked his daughter.

"Twenty-one weeks."

"Five months," her father said, converting the response. "You didn't say a single word to me about this for *five months*."

"I didn't know how to tell you, and I knew you'd have strong opinions about what we should do—"

"Damn right I do."

"And I know we have some decisions to make," Haylee continued, her tone placating. "But you have to let me and Trevor make them."

"How could you let this happen?" her father demanded, shaking his head. "You're a Gilmore and he's a Blake."

"What does that have to do with anything?"

"Everything, because the news that Trevor Blake knocked up Haylee Gilmore is going to get things all stirred up again."

"The only one getting stirred up is *you*," Haylee said.

"Speaking of stirring," Colleen said, returning with Finley and Logan in tow. "I need Haylee to help me in the kitchen with the gravy."

"Why are you asking her for help?" Logan teased. "She can't cook."

Haylee glared at her brother even as she rose to her feet to give him a hug. Of course, she hadn't told him about her pregnancy, either, and his eyes practically popped out of his head when he felt the roundness of her belly press against him.

"Whoa," he said. "Maybe you have learned to cook— and eat—because you've packed on more than a few pounds since I last saw you."

She smacked the back of his head playfully. "I'm pregnant, you moron."

"Wow. Um…" His gaze darted cautiously between his sister, their father and their guest. "Congratulations?"

"Thank you." She kissed his cheek. "I'm going to help Colleen in the kitchen."

He made a pained face. "And I was really looking forward to a delicious meal."

"I'll help, too," Finley said, grabbing her sister's arm as she lifted her hand to smack Logan again.

Haylee mouthed *sorry* to Trevor as she was dragged toward the kitchen.

Though he wished he could follow her, he held his ground and offered his hand to Haylee's brother. "I'm Trevor."

The younger man's gaze narrowed on him. "You're the baby's father?"

He nodded.

Logan's grip tightened painfully. "So when's the wedding?"

"We were just discussing that," Robert said.

And Trevor realized it was going to be a very long three days.

Chapter Seventeen

"I think that went pretty well," Trevor remarked, after they'd finished their meal and retreated to the carriage house, where he and Haylee were spending the weekend.

"Were we at the same table?" she asked incredulously.

"The meal was delicious."

"Colleen's a good cook," she agreed.

"And dessert was even better."

She smiled then. "Thanks. Though I noticed that you opted for pumpkin despite telling me you were dying to try the pecan."

"I saw the way your dad glowered at Logan when he asked for a slice of pecan, and I figured he already had enough reasons to want to kill me in my sleep."

"I'll make another pecan pie when we get back to Haven, just for you," she promised.

"I'll hold you to that," he said. "Now tell me what our plans are for tomorrow."

"I figured you'd be ready to leave at sunrise."

"I want you to enjoy this weekend with your family," he assured her.

"I'm not sure how much enjoyment is going to be had considering my dad's mood." She sighed. "Did you notice that he hardly spoke two words to me during dinner?"

"I'm sorry," he said sincerely.

She shrugged, ignoring the tears burning the backs of her eyes. "It's not your fault."

"Isn't it?"

"It takes two to tango," she pointed out.

"But I'm the one who asked you to dance."

She managed a smile. "Only literally," she said. "I'm the one who invited you back to my hotel room."

"You did," he confirmed. "And I don't regret a single minute of that night."

"Do you really mean that?" she asked dubiously.

"I really do," he said. "I know my initial reaction to the pregnancy left a lot to be desired, but that was just because it caught me completely off guard. Once I had some time to wrap my head around the idea that I was going to be a father, I realized it was something that I wanted. That our babies are wanted."

The sincerity in his tone had fresh tears welling in her eyes. "I was terrified by the idea of having to go through all of this on my own," she confided. "I'm so grateful to you for stepping up." Then she sighed. "And sorry that my dad can't be happy for us."

"He'll come around," Trevor said. "Though truthfully, I can understand why he's upset. If we have a girl—or girls—you can bet that she or they will be locked up until they're thirty."

"Thirty seems a little extreme."

"Look what happened to you at twenty-nine," he teased.

"Look what happened," she agreed, touching a hand to the curve of her belly.

He placed his hand over hers. "Colleen will bring your dad around," he said, hoping to reassure her. "She seems to have a way with him."

"She does," Haylee agreed with a nod. "But who's going to bring Elijah and Lorraine around?"

"That's a good question," he admitted. "Of course, getting married would likely help smooth things over with both sets of parents."

"Can we include that oh-so-romantic sentiment in our vows?"

"Sure," he agreed, ignoring her sarcasm. "Along with noting that we enjoy spending time together, we're both committed to being good parents and we share off-the-charts chemistry in the bedroom."

"We had sex *once*," she said dismissively. "You can't make a claim like that after only one night."

"I'm willing to put my claim to the test—anytime," he told her.

She shook her head. "You can't be the least bit attracted to me right now."

"Not the least bit," he agreed. "A whole lot."

"Are you one of those guys who's turned on by pregnant women?"

"I'm one of those guys who's turned on by *you*."

"You say things like that, and yet…"

"And yet?" he prompted.

She shook her head.

"And yet we've been living together for almost five weeks and I still haven't kissed you?" he guessed.

"That isn't what I was going to say," she told him, but her refusal to meet his gaze suggested that he'd hit pretty close to the truth. "You were pretty clear about the rules when I moved in with you."

"I said I wouldn't try to seduce you while you were living under my roof," he acknowledged, taking her face gently in his hands. "But we're not under my roof now, are we?"

And then he kissed her.

Finally, Haylee thought, as his mouth settled over hers.

But that was as far as things went before her sister walked into the room.

"Whoops!"

Of course, Haylee knew that if her sister hadn't wanted to interrupt, she would have turned back around and walked out of the room again without saying anything at all.

"Of course, annoying sisters wouldn't barge in under my roof," Trevor mock-whispered to her now.

"But this is *my* roof," Finley said unapologetically. "And I'm just getting a drink and then going back to my office—but please don't do anything that's going to traumatize Simon."

"When are we going home?" he asked, after Finley had gone.

Not soon enough.

"Sunday," she reminded him.

"If we'd thought about it, we could have made an appointment to see Dr. Robertson while we're here this weekend."

"Not likely."

"Why not?"

"Because it's not just a weekend, it's a holiday weekend."

"So when is your next appointment?" he asked.

"Actually, I'm not going to see Dr. Robertson again."

"You haven't decided to give birth at home with a midwife or something crazy like that, have you?"

She laughed. "For your information, midwives can deliver babies in hospitals, too. But no, I've only decided to continue my prenatal care with Dr. Amaro in Battle Mountain."

"Are you telling me…are you planning to stay in Haven?"

"Rohan said that he has work for me at least through January, if I want it. And by that time, I'll probably be ready for some time off to get ready for the babies' arrival," she explained. "Plus, I know you really want to be there for the delivery, and this seemed the most logical way to make it happen."

"I don't know what to say," he admitted. "So I'll start with thank you."

"Well, it's not just for you," she said. "I'd kind of like

you to be there, too, so that I have someone to swear at when I'm sweating through labor."

He grinned. "I'm your man."

The first time that Trevor proposed to Haylee, he was only trying to do the right thing. She'd been absolutely right about that. He hadn't given any real thought to what it would be like to marry a woman he didn't even know; he'd only been thinking that he had to step up and take responsibility for the consequences of his actions.

Beyond that, he also wanted his children to have the benefit of growing up with two parents. And he wanted to be a dad who was there for all the big and little milestones in their lives. He didn't want to be a weekend dad or—far worse, if Haylee decided to go back to California—an occasional-holiday-and-two-weeks-in-the-summer dad.

But now that she'd decided to stay in Haven at least until the babies were born, he was determined to take advantage of every minute to show her the kind of life they could have together as a family. And the upcoming holiday season fit perfectly into his plans.

"Tell me about your first high school crush," Trevor suggested, as they made their way to town square for the tree lighting ceremony the following Wednesday night.

"That seems like an oddly random request," she noted.

"The program of events for tonight said that the high school band would be there, which got me thinking about my own high school days and wondering about yours."

"Why do you assume I had a high school crush?"

"Because everyone does," he said matter-of-factly.

"Who was yours?" she asked.

He smiled at the memory. "Skylar Gilmore."

"You had a crush on my cousin?"

"Westmount High isn't a very big school and—" he shrugged "—her last name notwithstanding, she's really hot."

"She's also engaged to a Marine," Haylee pointed out to him.

"I saw the ring—and her fiancé—at your grandparents' anniversary party." He lifted his arm to flex his biceps. "Lucky for him, I got over my crush on his fiancée a long time ago."

"I'm sure he'd be shaking in his combat boots otherwise," she said, fighting against a smile.

"Now tell me about your crush," he urged.

"His name was Cory Ransom," she finally said. "He had shaggy blond hair that was always falling into his eyes and the sweetest smile."

"Was he a jock, stoner or geek?"

She frowned at the labels. "He played bass clarinet in the band and served as treasurer on student council."

"Definitely a geek," Trevor decided.

"If he was, then so was I."

"Did he ever find out about your crush? Was he secretly crushing on you, too?"

"Yes and no," she said. "Although, for almost two full weeks in my senior year, I was foolish enough to believe that he liked me, too."

"What happened?"

"He asked me to be his date for the spring formal."

"Sounds like a pretty good reason to believe he liked you," Trevor noted.

"I was so excited," she confided. "Especially since he'd always seemed more interested in my sister than me. But I didn't clue in, not even when he suggested that we share a limo with Finley and her date—" Her brow furrowed. "I can't even remember who she went to prom with that year. Damon? Calvin? Brian?" Then she nodded. "It was Brian Nardone."

Of course, the name meant nothing to Trevor, so she continued. "Anyway, I found out later that Cory only asked me to go with him because Finley had already agreed to go with Brian, and he figured that double-dating with them meant he'd still get to spend the evening with her."

"Ouch."

She nodded.

"How'd you find out?"

"I saw my date putting the moves on my sister. Of course, Finley had some moves of her own and dropped him with a quick jab to his nose."

"For real?"

She nodded. "He fell to his knees, apologizing to her. She told him that he should be apologizing to me."

"Did he?"

"If you consider 'I'm-sorry-but-you-should-have-known-that-I-really-wanted-to-be-with-your-sister' an apology," she said.

"Were you heartbroken?"

"Less than I thought I'd be, because I think I always knew he wasn't interested in me. But I was disappointed. And embarrassed."

"Where's this guy now? What's he doing with his life?"

"I have no idea."

"Then how am I supposed to find him and punch him in the nose?"

"Finley already took care of that," she reminded him.

"That doesn't make me feel any better."

"While I appreciate your Neanderthal instincts, I got over my crush on Cory a long time ago."

"That helps," he decided, as they joined the crowd gathered around the big tree in the center of the square.

It seemed as if most of the town had turned out for the big event, including the high school band, as Trevor had noted, playing classic holiday tunes, and the children's choir, singing along. The Rotary Club was selling hot chocolate in support of Toys for Tots and accepting canned food donations on behalf of the local food bank.

Trevor stood behind her, his arms around her to insulate her from the biting wind, while the mayor gave a thankfully brief speech that talked about the spirit of the season and the importance of helping others—not just during the holidays but throughout the year. He finished by wishing a "Merry Christmas" to all and lighting the tree.

The crowd gasped as the tree was illuminated, red and green and blue lights shining brightly against the darkness of night, and Trevor whispered, "Good job," close to Haylee's ear.

She tipped her head back to smile at him then. "I cursed that tree the whole while that I was fumbling with tangled lights, but now, yeah, I can agree that it was all worthwhile."

The frigid air had turned her cheeks and nose pink, but her lips were curved and her eyes sparkled, and looking at her, Trevor felt something shift inside his heart. And in that moment, the man who'd been certain he wasn't capable of experiencing love again, knew he was in serious danger of falling for this woman.

"Can we go home now?" she asked.

It pleased him that she'd started referring to his house as "home," but he knew better than to draw her attention to the fact.

"Yes," he said. "We can go home now."

When they got there, he took her coat to hang it in the closet, his hand brushing against hers in the exchange.

"Your hands are like ice," he noted.

"Because it's freezing outside."

He sandwiched her cold hands between his much larger and warmer ones.

"You need better gloves," he decided.

"Or hot chocolate?" she suggested hopefully.

"I can make hot chocolate," he said. "But why don't we try something else first?"

He slid his arms around her and drew her close—or as close as her growing belly would allow, then lowered his head and touched his mouth to hers.

His lips moved over hers softly, fleetingly, savoring the moment. He loved kissing her, loved the way her lips yielded and her body melted. He loved the quiet sounds she made deep in her throat.

But he wanted more than a few stolen kisses. He wanted to make love with her again, to enjoy not just the taste of her lips but the mating of their bodies. But he was trying to take things slow this time—trying to show some of the patience and finesse that had been lacking the first time he'd taken her to bed.

Her first time ever with a man.

He couldn't make up for the mistakes he'd made, but he could ensure that the next time was better. And he would, if he ever got the chance.

"I think that did the trick," she said, when he eased his lips from hers.

"I'm glad," he said, and brushed his mouth over hers again. "Do you still want hot chocolate?"

She lifted her gaze to his. "What are my other options?"

"Anything you want."

"I want you," she admitted.

"That's convenient," he said. "Because I want you, too."

"I don't understand why," she admitted softly. "Especially now—"

He touched a finger to her lips, silencing her doubts.

He didn't know the root of her insecurity, but he knew it ran deep. Perhaps it had started with the abandonment by her mother and been exacerbated by the popularity of her more outgoing sister. Whatever the reason, he couldn't go back in time and change any of that for her, he could only assure her that right now, she was everything he wanted.

"I want you because you're smart and beautiful, strong and sexy, compassionate and stubborn, kind and generous, and every day that I spend with you, I only want you more."

"Show me that you want me," she said. "Take me to bed."

"Your wish is my command," he said, and lifted her effortlessly into his arms to carry her to his bedroom.

He set her on her feet beside the bed, then kissed her again. His tongue swept into her mouth, tasting, teasing. His hands slid under her top, touching, tempting.

She wasn't sure what to do with her own hands. She wanted to touch him, too, but considering the way the world was tilting beneath her feet, she was afraid that if she let go of his shoulders, she'd tumble to the floor.

He eased his mouth from hers to whisk her sweater over her head. Her long-sleeved undershirt and bra followed. She shivered as the cool air brushed over her skin.

"I'll keep you warm," he promised, as he eased her back onto the mattress and tugged her leggings and panties over her hips, down her legs, and tossed them aside with the other discarded garments.

"I'm not cold anymore," she told him.

Because she wasn't.

Because how could she be cold when there was so much heat flooding her system?

He got rid of his own clothes, then straddled her naked body, his knees bracketing her hips, holding her in position while his hands and mouth moved over her, exploring and exciting her with every touch.

"Your breasts are fuller," he noted, cupping them almost reverently in his palms. "Are they more sensitive?"

"*Everything* is more sensitive."

He smiled at that. "This might be even more fun than I anticipated."

"Have you been anticipating this?"

"Every night since you moved in," he said, then he

shook his head. "No. Every night since we first made love."

He knew just where to focus his attention to maximize her pleasure, and though she understood that his knowledge was the result of a wealth of experience, she refused to dwell on that now. She refused to compare herself to the undoubtedly numerous women who'd shared his bed before her.

She was only going to focus on the here and now.

And here and now, her body was quivering with wanting.

Since she didn't have the same wealth of experience, she let her instincts guide her as she reached between their bodies and wrapped her fingers around him. She felt him jerk in her hand, and immediately released her grip.

"I'm sorry."

"No." His fingers circled her wrist, drawing her hand back to him, encouraging her exploration. "It's good." His eyes closed on a groan as she stroked him. "Really good."

Then he lowered his head and kissed her again, long and slow and deep. His hands continued to move over her, stoking the fire that burned deep inside her.

She'd always been a sucker for romantic books and movies, but as much as she'd enjoyed watching or reading about a couple finding their way toward a happily-ever-after, she'd been suspicious of the love scenes. Heroines who'd never truly known physical satisfaction until they gave themselves to the fictional heroes.

She'd had no great expectations when she'd invited Trevor back to her hotel room after the wedding. She'd just wanted to know what all the hype was about, but she hadn't expected to feel the earth move. She hadn't anticipated that her body would be capable of feeling so much—and somehow still yearn for more.

He'd given her everything she wanted—and more.

She'd been stunned and breathless and perhaps a little bit scared. She wasn't accustomed to being out of control, but from the first kiss, the first touch, there was no denying that he was in command.

It was no different this time. From the first brush of his hands, the first touch of his lips, she was at his mercy. But at least she knew what to expect this time, or so she thought until he shifted his position on the mattress as his hands stroked her body and his mouth moved lower, trailing kisses over the swell of her abdomen, nibbling the inside of her thighs.

Her breath caught in her throat when he gently nudged her knees farther apart and settled between them. He parted the soft folds of flesh at the apex of her thighs, and everything inside her tensed and tightened. Then his tongue flicked over the nub at her center, a playful stroke that made her gasp even as her hips instinctively lifted off the mattress.

He responded to the wordless request, continuing to lick and nibble and suck until she was sure she couldn't take any more.

Still, he gave more.

"Please," she said. "I can't…"

She didn't know what she intended to say, but he wasn't listening to her, anyway.

She flew apart—shattering into a million jagged little pieces like the explosion of a light bulb that had absorbed too much current.

He held her as she came back to earth, her body quivering and trembling. And he brushed his lips gently over hers then. "Okay?"

She could only nod as he finally moved into position between her thighs, filling and fulfilling her. The tension immediately began to build inside her again, even before he started to move, long and steady strokes that caused the pressure to build ever higher. Then deeper. Harder. Faster.

Her fingers dug into his shoulders, holding on to him as the world tilted and spun. She could tell that he was close to his release. She could hear it in the shallowness of his breathing, feel it in the tense muscles of his arms as he held himself over her.

He seemed to be holding himself back, waiting for something…waiting for her? But he'd already given her so much pleasure. So much more than she'd expected or anticipated.

And still there was more yet again.

When he finally let himself go, she knew that he'd taken more than just her body this time—he'd taken her heart.

Chapter Eighteen

Trevor fell asleep with Haylee in his arms, and she was still there when he awakened the next morning. He wasn't accustomed to sharing his bed, and he was surprised to realize that he didn't mind her being there. No, it was more than that — he wanted her there. Not just this morning but every morning, for the rest of their lives together.

He'd already thought about making the room directly across the hall into a nursery, so it would be easy for them to hear and tend to the babies when they needed anything. Though she hadn't said anything about staying in Haven long-term, he refused to consider any other possibility. And he hoped that, after last night, she'd realize their babies were only one of the many reasons she should stay.

She shifted in her sleep, sliding her leg over top of his, snuggling so that her breasts were pressed against his chest. Yeah, he could definitely get used to falling asleep with Haylee in his arms and waking up with her beside him. And because she was there, and conveniently naked, he let his hand skim from her thigh to her hip to her breast. He loved the softness of her skin, the curves of her body, the roundness of her belly where their twin babies nestled in her womb. He found her breast, brushed his thumb over her nipple. She sighed softly, then her eyelids flickered and slowly lifted.

"Good morning," he said.

"Good morning," she echoed, a little shyly.

"Did you sleep well?"

"Very well," she said. "And you?"

"Same." He dipped his head to brush his mouth over hers.

Her eyelids drifted shut again as he deepened the kiss. And when he shifted so that she was beneath him, she opened for him not just willingly but eagerly, and their bodies began to move, finding their rhythm and release together.

"You had sex," Finley said, during a Skype call with her sister the following afternoon.

"I'm almost six months pregnant and it wasn't an immaculate conception, so why do you sound surprised?" Haylee wondered.

"I mean you had sex recently," her sister clarified.

"How could you possibly know something like that?" she demanded.

"You have a definite glow, and before you remind me again that you're six months pregnant, I'll point out that you weren't glowing quite so much when we chatted just a few days ago."

"Okay, yes. I had sex."

"Now hold up your hands."

"What? Why?"

"Because I want to see the ring."

Haylee sighed and shook her head. "You're almost as pushy as he is."

"So there's no ring?" her sister asked, sounding disappointed.

"There's no ring."

"I don't understand," Finley said. "Why are you still refusing to make wedding plans when it's obvious that you're head over heels in love with the guy?"

She didn't bother to deny it. Her sister had always been able to read her like an open book. "It's not my feelings that are in question," she said.

"You doubt his feelings for you?"

No, she had no reason to doubt his feelings. She knew exactly what they were and what they weren't. He cared about her, but he didn't love her, and he'd made it clear that he never would.

And she couldn't marry a man who didn't love her.

"Take a leap," Finley urged. "Tell him how you feel."

"I'll think about it," Haylee said, but only to get her sister off her back.

Because the truth was, she had no intention of leaping and going splat.

* * *

"Hey," Haylee immediately protested, when Trevor pulled back the heavy curtains, filling the room with bright sunlight. "It's Saturday."

"It is," he agreed.

"I get to sleep in on Saturday."

"And you did."

She reluctantly opened one eye even as she pulled the covers up under her chin. "What time is it?"

"Eleven thirty."

She jolted upright. "It is not. It can't be."

He pointed to the clock beside the bed.

"I honestly don't remember the last time I slept so late," she told him.

"I didn't want to wake you, but the farm closes at three o'clock."

"Farm?" she echoed dubiously. "Like with cows and pigs and stuff?"

He smiled. "Like with Christmas trees."

"Really?" There was joy in that single word and light in her eyes.

"Really," he confirmed. "If you can be ready in half an hour, we'll even stop for lunch on the way."

"I can be ready," she promised.

True to her word, twenty-nine minutes later she was tucking her feet into her boots. Trevor was more interested in the rest of her and noted with appreciation the denim leggings and knit turtleneck sweater that hugged her curves.

He'd never been one of those guys who thought all pregnant women were beautiful or that they glowed from the marvel of life growing inside them. Maybe it was because Haylee was carrying his babies, but Trevor thought she looked stunning.

They grabbed a quick bite at the Sunnyside Diner, because despite it being lunchtime, Haylee wanted breakfast. After they'd fueled up with pancakes and sausage, they headed toward Comet's Christmas Tree Farm, fifteen miles past the Dusty Boots Motel on the highway leading out of town.

"Did your family come here to get Christmas trees when you were a kid?" Haylee asked, as he helped her out of the truck.

"Nah. We usually just chopped one down at Crooked Creek," he told her. "But this is the top-rated local Christmas tree farm on Yelp."

"Out of how many?" she wondered.

"One," he admitted. "But the reviews were all positive."

She started toward a fenced-in area beneath a banner that advertised Precut Trees arranged in groups by height. But Trevor caught her shoulders and turned her in the opposite direction.

"If we're going to get a tree, we're going to get the whole tree experience."

She glanced at the signs that guided visitors toward the Cut Your Own Tree section.

"Did you bring anything to cut a tree with?"

"Didn't have to." He pointed toward a covered market-style stand, the back wall of which was hung with saws of various sizes. "We can borrow what we need, including a sled to haul the tree back with us."

"Then what are we waiting for? Let's go get a tree," she said.

After he'd signed out the required tools, they headed toward the self-serve section of the farm. There were several other couples and families wandering through the trees, discussing and debating options. Despite some heated disagreements about color and size, it was readily apparent to Haylee that this was a happy tradition for everyone there.

She paused when she spotted a man and woman with a couple of little boys who might have been twins—seven or eight years old, she guessed. The mom stood on the sidelines, her mitten-clad hands wrapped around a travel mug, watching as the dad helped the boys saw through the trunk of the tree they'd selected.

"Look, Mom!" the boy in the dark blue coat called out. "We're doing it."

"We're cutting the tree," his brother, wearing a matching gray coat, added.

"I'm looking," she promised. "You're doing a great job."

"When we go see Santa, can we tell him we cut the tree?"

"Of course."

"And then we can tell him what we want for Christmas, right?"

"You can tell him about *one* thing on your wish list," she said. "But remember, he's got a lot of gifts to deliver to a lot of kids, so there are no guarantees."

"But we were *really* good this year."

"Except when you were fighting," the boys' dad chimed in.

"Yeah. 'Cept when we were fighting."

"Haylee?"

Still smiling at the exchange, she hurried to catch up with Trevor again.

"Did your family go out into the woods hunting for the perfect tree when you were a kid?" he asked, as they walked around the lot, examining various specimens.

She shook her head. "We went to the local hardware store and picked a tree from the lot."

"Well, it's kind of the same thing," he said. "So take a look around and tell me which tree you think will look best in the living room."

"Where, in the living room, are you planning to put it?"

He shrugged. "Beside the sofa, maybe."

She wrinkled her nose.

"Or a much better location that you're going to suggest," he said dryly.

"I was just thinking, if you put it beside the fireplace, you'd be able to see it when you're sitting on the sofa," she pointed out.

"Okay, we'll put it beside the fireplace," he agreed.

She liked the way he said "we," as if she and Trevor really were a "we"—even if it was only a temporary situation.

"But then you'll have to move the recliner."

"So I'll move the recliner," he said. "No one ever sits there anyway."

"True," she acknowledged.

"Now we know where it's going, but we still have to pick the tree." He pointed to one nearby. "How about that one?"

She looked at the tree, then at him. "It's perfect...

if you're looking for a prop to stage a production of *A Charlie Brown Christmas*."

He perused the tree more closely. "I guess it is a little sparse," he acknowledged.

"And crooked."

"What about this one?" he asked, moving on to the next evergreen.

She did a slow walk around the specimen. "I think it could work."

He retrieved the saw from the sled.

"Is there anything I can do to help?" Haylee asked.

"Stay out of the way, so the tree doesn't fall on top of you."

"I can do that," she agreed.

She could also appreciate the scenery—and she indulged herself in doing just that. Whether he was wearing chinos with a shirt and tie to go to the office or jeans and flannel to hang out at home, Trevor always looked good. Today, in deference to their outdoor venture, he was wearing a leather jacket over a chunky knit sweater and well-worn jeans that hugged his thighs and butt. Even through the various layers of clothing, she couldn't help but appreciate the breadth of his shoulders and the power of his muscles as he sawed through the trunk of the tree they'd chosen.

And yet despite his obvious strength, he'd been a patient and selfless lover, ensuring that she experienced a pleasure she hadn't even known existed. Which was definitely something she should *not* be thinking about right now, she realized, as her blood warmed and her body temperature began to rise.

She unzipped her coat and loosened the soft wool

scarf she'd wrapped around her throat in an effort to cool the heat in her veins.

When the tree was strapped down on the sled, they retraced their steps toward the sales office to finalize their purchase.

The young man working at the toolshed measured their tree and gave them a slip, directing them to the barn to complete their purchase.

Haylee had been so focused on finding a tree that she hadn't even glanced toward the barn when they arrived. But she did so now, and noted that the wide doors were flanked by potted fir trees wrapped in red ribbon and decorated with shiny red balls. Evergreen boughs were tacked over the entranceway and similarly decked out.

The inside didn't look much like a shelter for livestock. The space was open and brightly lit, with signs hanging from the rafters to identify designated areas, such as Craft Corner and Cookies & Cider.

Curious, she took a few steps toward the Craft Corner where a teenager, dressed like an elf, was sitting at a child-sized picnic table with a couple of young children, helping them decorate paper plate wreaths. At another table, a trio of preschoolers were occupied with fat crayons and holiday-themed coloring pages. The on-site activity center was obviously designed to keep kids occupied while their parents browsed in the gift shop at the back.

Looking around, she noticed that all the employees of Comet's Christmas Tree Farm were dressed like Santa's helpers, complete with jingle bells on their shoes and pointy hats on their heads.

Haylee breathed in the scent of pine and… "Do I smell apples?"

"Hot apple cider," he said, nudging her toward the area designated Cookies & Cider. "Do you want a cup?"

"Yes, please."

He held up two fingers to the young woman—also dressed like an elf—who was stirring the spiced cider in an enormous pot. She ladled a portion into each of two cups, then passed them across the counter.

"Enjoy," she said, with a smile. "And make sure you try the cookies, too. They're made fresh every day."

"Try the cookies," Trevor repeated to Haylee.

She surveyed the artfully arranged assortment. "I shouldn't."

"Why not?"

"Because I've already gained twenty pounds."

"Those twenty pounds look good on you."

"You're only saying that because half of them are spilling out of my bra."

He had to fight the smile that wanted to tug at his lips. "Are they? I hadn't noticed."

"Liar."

He was chuckling as an older woman with gray hair neatly secured in a bun at the nape of her neck and wire-rimmed glasses perched on her nose came over to replenish the display of cookies.

"Mrs. Claus?" Haylee guessed.

"Oh no, dear," she said, with a conspiratorial wink. "Mrs. Claus is at the North Pole, helping Santa get ready for Christmas. We're just some of Santa's happy helpers here." She tapped the tag fastened to her red vest. "I'm Meg."

"Did you make these cookies, Meg?" Trevor asked, selecting another from the tray. "Because they're delicious."

She nodded. "I did."

"Spritz cookies are one of my holiday favorites," Haylee said, giving in to temptation and reaching for one in the shape of a snowflake sprinkled with blue sugar. "But the shapes never hold for me when I make them."

"Because no one ever told you the secret trick," Meg guessed. Then she dropped her voice to a whisper and said, "Chilled cookie sheets."

"Really?"

The older woman nodded. "I promise, it makes all the difference."

"I'll give it a try," Haylee said.

"But right now, we need to pay for our tree," Trevor said, brushing cookie crumbs off his fingers.

"Did you get a receipt from Lewis at the toolshed?"

Trevor pulled it out of his jacket pocket.

"The cash register's in the gift shop," Meg said.

"Of course," he said. "Just like at Disneyland—exit through the gift shop."

The older woman smiled. "In addition to trees, we've got everything you need to decorate them and your home. We also have a variety of personalized ornaments, handcrafted gifts and toys."

"I'm going to take another cookie and go do some shopping."

But as they made their way around the gift shop, it was Trevor who seemed to be on a mission.

"What are you planning to do with all those lights?"

Haylee asked, as he dropped several packages into his basket.

"Put them on the tree."

"You don't think you have enough at home?"

"I don't actually have any," he admitted. "I've never put up a tree or decorated for the holidays before."

"Why not?"

"Because I usually spend Christmas Day at my parents' house."

"But what about all the days and nights before the holidays?" she asked.

He shrugged. "It just always seemed like more bother than it was worth."

"So why is this year different?"

"Because I want our first Christmas together to be perfect."

Our first Christmas.

Haylee liked the sound of that.

But still, she was afraid to hope.

"Look at these," he said, holding up two knitted stockings in traditional Nordic designs. One was blue with snowflakes and mittens and the other was red with Christmas trees and reindeer.

"For the babies?" she guessed.

He nodded.

"They're certainly big enough for Santa to fill with lots of goodies."

He grinned. "That's what I was thinking. There are green and gray ones, too," he told her. "Maybe we should get one in each color."

Of course they'd need four stockings for their babies, she realized. One set for Christmas at Mommy's house and one set for Christmas at Daddy's. And though she knew he was only being practical—maybe even thoughtful—the reality of their situation put a sudden pall on what had been, up to that point, a near-perfect day.

"Haylee?" he prompted.

She had to clear the tightness from her throat before she could reply. "Sure. One of each would be good."

Then she turned away, feigning an interest in the pine cone ornaments displayed on one of the many tabletop trees set up around the shop.

"What do you think?" Trevor asked, after he'd finished securing the trunk into the base that they'd also bought at the Christmas tree farm. He tilted his head. "Is it crooked?"

"It's perfect. Or it will be, when you put all the lights and ornaments on it that you bought at the tree farm."

"What was in all those packages you bought?" he asked.

"I got handmade ornaments for Colleen, Finley, my grandmother and—because it was irresistible, a dated 'Baby's First Christmas' ornament for Colton."

"You obviously believe in getting an early start on your shopping," he noted.

"You think this is early?" she asked incredulously.

"It's barely December."

"It *is* December," she said. "And Christmas is less than three weeks away."

He shrugged, obviously unconcerned. "It doesn't take long to buy gift cards."

"That's the extent of your Christmas shopping? Gift cards?"

"What's wrong with gift cards?" he wanted to know.

"Nothing," she said, though her tone suggested otherwise. "They're a perfectly acceptable gift for a co-worker or pet sitter or mail carrier, but not your parents or brother or grandfather."

Or girlfriend-slash-fiancée-slash-wife, he guessed, though she didn't mention any of those.

"I've never heard any complaints."

She shook her head. "Why don't you skip the card purchase and just wrap the cash? Better yet, save the wrapping and use Venmo."

"This seems to be a hot button for you," he noted. "Did your ex-boyfriend give you a gift card last Christmas?"

"No," she denied. "Although that would be a valid reason for the shift of status from boyfriend to ex."

"Note to self—buy Haylee an actual present."

"That's not what I meant," she protested.

"You don't want a gift?"

She huffed out a breath. "Can we get back to focusing on the tree?"

"Sure," he agreed. "I'll start with the lights while you pop the corn."

"No one actually strings popcorn anymore," she told him.

He chuckled. "It's not for stringing. It's for eating. Decorating is hungry work."

He was right, and the big bowl of popcorn she made was empty long before they'd hung the last ornament on the tree. But still there were more holiday decorations to be put up, including the stockings Trevor had bought.

"Which one do you want?" he asked, holding them up for her inspection again.

"You're letting me choose?"

"Sure."

"I'll take the red and the green, if you don't mind."

"The traditional Christmas colors," he noted. "I always suspected that you were a traditional girl at heart, but you only get one—so is it red or green?"

She frowned at that. "Why do I only get one?"

"Why do you need more than one?"

She sensed that there was a miscommunication happening and was eager to clarify. "Didn't you get four so that we'd each have a set for the babies?"

He dropped his arms. "That's what you thought?" he asked, sounding surprised—and maybe a little bit disappointed.

"What else was I supposed to think?" she said.

"That there will be four of *us*—you, me and two babies."

"Oh."

He shook his head. "Apparently I'm the only one of us who hopes that our first Christmas together isn't also our last."

She didn't know what to say to that—she had no experience with relationships. She knew she'd hurt him, however inadvertently, but she didn't know how to make it right. And before she could come up with a reply, she heard the back door slam.

He was gone.

And she was left behind. Again.

Chapter Nineteen

Haylee halted abruptly in midstride when she walked into the kitchen the following morning and spotted Trevor leaning against the counter, drinking a cup of coffee.

She looked tired, he noted, as if she hadn't slept well—or maybe not much at all.

If so, that made two of them.

Recovering her composure, she moved to the cupboard to retrieve a mug. He automatically flipped the switch on the electric kettle, to heat the water for the peppermint tea she liked to drink in the morning.

"I didn't realize you were here," she finally said.

"I do live here," he reminded her.

"You walked out," she said, accusation in her tone.

"I was mad," he pointed out in his defense. "And I didn't want to say something I would regret later."

"You walked out," she repeated.

The way she said it reminded him of the words she'd used to describe the circumstances of her parents' separation: *She walked out and never came back*.

And he realized how deeply scarred she'd been by her mother's abandonment.

"But I came back," he said gently. "And no matter how upset or angry I might get when we argue about something, I'll always come back."

"How can you be so sure?" The question was barely more than a whisper.

And he realized that what she really wanted to know was how could *she* be sure.

"Because I can't imagine my life without you in it," he said sincerely.

Inexplicably her eyes filled with tears.

"Hey," he said, gently brushing her hair away from her face.

"I don't want our first Christmas together to be our last," she told him, the words pouring out in a rush. "But I don't want to get my hopes up, either."

He took her hands and gently pulled her into his arms. "Then maybe we should agree to take it one day at a time," he suggested.

"I can do that." She leaned her forehead against his chest. "I don't like to fight."

"Me, neither, but the making up could be fun. And look at that—you're standing under the mistletoe."

She tipped her head back to see a sprig of holiday

greenery hanging from the ceiling. "When did you put that up there?"

"The *when* doesn't matter," he told her. "All that matters is that you're under it and now I have to kiss you."

"I don't think that's actually a rule," she said.

"Maybe it's not a rule, but it *is* considered bad luck to refuse a kiss under the mistletoe."

"Well, I certainly don't want bad luck."

"Then let's make sure you don't get it," he said, and lowered his mouth to touch hers.

It felt as if it had been weeks instead of hours since she'd been in his arms, and Haylee immediately realized that there was nowhere else she wanted to be. But she didn't just love the way he made her feel—she loved *him*.

He was handsome and kind and interesting and funny and an amazing lover. Plus he didn't seem to mind that she was a lousy cook, or that she didn't bother with makeup or even that she was more comfortable in steel-toed boots than high-heeled shoes.

He accepted her just the way she was. And that was everything she'd never known she was looking for.

"Hungry?" he asked, when he finally eased his mouth from hers.

And bonus—he liked to feed her.

"Starving," she admitted, with a smile.

"Go get dressed while I start breakfast."

"Or...you could help me get dressed and we could eat breakfast later?" she suggested hopefully.

"A much better plan," he decided.

* * *

Haylee knew that if she walked back to her car and drove away now, no one would ever need to know that she'd been here. Except maybe whoever was monitoring the half a dozen security cameras that were focused on the front door. Instead she drew in a deep breath and splayed a hand on her belly.

"I'm doing this for you guys. Because I want you to have a good relationship with both sides of your family."

And because she knew that wouldn't happen unless someone took a first step, she lifted a hand and knocked on the heavy wood.

When the door opened, she was taken aback to see Lorraine Blake on the other side of the threshold.

"Haylee…this is a surprise." Trevor's mom sounded not just surprised but pleased to see her.

"I should have called first," she acknowledged. In fact, she'd thought about doing so but had opted for a spontaneous visit—in case she chickened out at the last minute.

"Don't be silly," Lorraine said. "You're welcome to drop by anytime."

Haylee couldn't imagine this would ever become a habit, but she appreciated the sentiment. "I won't take much of your time," she promised.

"But you will come in for a cup of tea, won't you? I just put the kettle on and it would be nice to have some company."

"Oh. Um. Sure."

Lorraine smiled and stepped away from the door so that she could enter. "Let me take your coat."

So much for making a quick getaway, Haylee thought, as she unbuttoned the garment.

"Thank you," she said, as Lorraine hung it in the closet.

"What kind of tea do you like?" Trevor's mom was already on her way to the kitchen, leaving Haylee with no choice but to follow. "I've heard that Rooibos is good during pregnancy, because of its antioxidant properties."

"Please don't go to any trouble on my account."

"It's no trouble at all. And that's the kettle starting to whistle now."

So Haylee took a seat at the granite island in the spacious kitchen while Lorraine made tea.

"There should be some cookies here, too," Trevor's mom said, opening and closing cupboards. "But Greta's out running errands and I have no idea where she keeps— oh, there they are." She opened a snap-lock container. "Do you like oatmeal chocolate chip?"

Haylee nodded.

"They're Trevor's favorite," Lorraine noted, as she arranged several cookies on a plate.

She set the plate near Haylee, then poured the tea. "Milk or sugar?"

"No, black is fine, thanks."

"I like mine the same way," Lorraine said. "Lots of cream and sugar in my coffee, but nothing in my tea." She sat down beside Haylee and offered a weak smile. "I'm babbling—I do that when I'm excited or nervous, and I have to confess to feeling a little of both because I don't know why you're here but I'm so glad that you are."

"You are?" Haylee asked cautiously.

"Let me start with an apology," Trevor's mom said. "I was rude and dismissive the first time I met you, partly because I was hurt and annoyed to hear through the office grapevine that my son was living with a woman he'd never even introduced to me, and partly because, well, even if you had royal blood rather than Gilmore blood in your veins, you still wouldn't be good enough for my son. And I know that sounds harsh, but when your children are old enough to date, you'll understand."

Haylee took a tentative sip of her tea as Lorraine continued to talk.

"Then I followed up by inviting you to our home but doing nothing to make you feel welcome." She took a cookie from the plate and broke it in half over a napkin. "I didn't know that Elijah was going to offer you money to go back to California…but I'm not sure I would have tried to talk him out of it if I did. And while I know his offer was crass and offensive, we both needed to know that you were with Trevor for the right reasons."

"I might have been able to appreciate the rationale if not for the execution," Haylee said. "Because while I was the target of the ambush, Trevor got caught up in it, too, and we both got hurt."

"I know, and I *am* sorry," Lorraine said now. "We both are. And you certainly don't owe us anything, but…we'd really like a chance to get to know you."

Haylee honestly didn't know what had happened to change Trevor's mom's attitude toward her, but there was no denying that she sounded sincere. And maybe the reasons weren't as important as the results, anyway. "I'd like that, too."

Lorraine smiled, obviously relieved. "Now that I got that off my chest, why don't you tell me why you stopped by?"

Haylee reached into the side pocket of her purse and pulled out a black-and-white photo. "I wanted to drop this off for you."

"What is—oh." The other woman's eyes got misty as she realized: "It's a picture of the babies."

She nodded. "Dr. Amaro wanted to do another ultrasound, just to double-check that both babies are developing on schedule—and they are," she assured the soon-to-be grandmother.

"How are you doing? Are you feeling good?"

"Mostly." To anyone else, she might have confessed that it was tiring to cart around an extra twenty pounds and frustrating to not be able to sleep on her back anymore, but she couldn't imagine she'd ever be comfortable sharing those kinds of personal details with Trevor's mom—and definitely not yet.

As the back door opened, Lorraine said, "That sounds like Elijah coming home."

Haylee forced a smile as she lifted her cup to her lips again.

Her plan had been to drop off the photo and leave—a gesture to hopefully open the lines of communication. She hadn't anticipated a tête-à-tête with Trevor's mom, and she certainly didn't want another confrontation with his dad. But she could hardly rush off when she still had half a cup of tea to drink.

"Who's car is…" Elijah's words trailed off when he saw Haylee sitting in his kitchen.

"Hello, Mr. Blake."

He nodded, an acknowledgment more than a greeting. But he didn't seem aloof so much as chastened, as if whatever had swayed Lorraine's attitude had similarly affected her husband, too.

"Look what Haylee brought for us, Elijah." Lorraine slid the picture across the counter for his perusal.

His face softened as he examined the image, the babies labeled Twin A and Twin B. He cleared his throat. "Did you find out if they're boys or girls or one of each?"

"We did," Haylee confirmed. "But Trevor isn't ready to tell anyone else yet."

"Are you going to do one of those gender reveal parties?" Lorraine asked hopefully. "We could host a little get-together here, if you wanted."

She shook her head. "Thanks, but we're not going to have a party."

"Maybe a baby shower? Babies need a lot of stuff, and two babies will need twice as much."

"We're going furniture shopping tomorrow," Haylee said. "Now that we've picked out the paint, Trevor's eager to get the room ready for the babies' arrival."

"Then it's good you stopped by today," Elijah said. "Because I've got something for you, too."

He wasn't gone more than half a minute before returning with a check that he set beside Haylee's cup.

"Déjà vu," she murmured.

"No," he said. "It's not—" He blew out a breath and looked helplessly at his wife.

"Elijah's trying to say he's sorry, too," Lorraine said.

"Then what's this?" Haylee asked.

But the answer was right there, on the memo line where her finger was pointing: to decorate the nursery.

It was a ridiculous amount of money, no doubt enough to decorate and furnish a whole house.

But Haylee realized that it was also an olive branch, so she took it—for Trevor's sake and for their babies.

A few days later, Trevor was assembling the cribs they'd bought for the nursery when Devin stopped by.

"Great—you can give me a hand," he said, gesturing for his brother to hold the end panel. "This is definitely a two-person job."

"Where's Haylee today?"

"At the spa with Brie and Regan. She claims she can't reach her feet anymore so she needs someone else to paint her toenails for her."

"Her belly does seem bigger every time I see her," Devin remarked.

"Do me a favor? Don't mention that to Haylee."

His brother chuckled. "She's been spending a fair amount of time with our cousins recently."

"And her own," Trevor said. "I know she misses Finley, but I think she's enjoying being here and getting to know her extended family better."

"I heard you guys had an appointment with her new doctor in Battle Mountain."

Trevor nodded. "Dr. Amaro who, coincidentally, delivered Regan's twins. But how did you hear about that?"

"Actually, Mom showed me a copy of the last ultrasound photo."

Trevor swore as the screwdriver slipped in his hand. "How did she get a copy of the photo?"

"Haylee dropped it off yesterday."

"So that's where she went," he realized. "She said she had some errands to run, but she didn't mention stopping by Mom and Dad's place." He shook his head. "I don't know if she's incredibly brave or incredibly foolish."

"I don't know, either," Devin admitted. "But I'd say you're incredibly lucky to have a woman who's willing to walk into the lion's den to make peace with your family."

"Yeah," Trevor agreed. "So is that why you stopped by—to tell me how lucky I am?"

Devin picked up the other end panel and held it in place so his brother could connect it to the sides.

"No. I wanted to let you know that I've got a couple of tickets to the Golden Knights game next Saturday night."

"Where'd you get your hands on those?"

"I did some work for a guy down there and, as a bonus, he gave me the tickets. I thought maybe we could make a weekend of it, if you're available."

"Sounds good," Trevor said.

"Just like that? You don't want to check with Haylee first?"

"She's not my wife," he reminded his brother.

"I hit a sore spot," Devin realized.

"Nope," he denied. "If she doesn't want to get married, I can hardly force her."

"I'm a little surprised to hear that she's still resisting. The last time I saw you guys together, you seemed totally in sync."

"I thought so, too, but apparently having a great relationship and wanting to raise our kids together isn't enough without love."

"So tell her that you love her," his brother urged.

"I'm not going to lie to her so that she'll let me put a ring on her finger."

"Now I see the problem," Devin said, shaking his head.

"Want to share?" he asked.

"You're an idiot."

"On second thought, you can keep your not-so-insightful opinions to yourself," Trevor decided.

"I didn't suggest that you lie to Haylee. I told you to tell her you love her because you do," his brother continued, not keeping his opinion to himself.

"But I don't."

"And the fact that you actually believe that is why you're an idiot."

"Look, Haylee's great. We get along well and I enjoy being with her, but I'm not stupid enough to open up my heart and fall in love again."

"Yeah, because that's something you can totally control," his brother said dryly.

"It is," he insisted.

"And so, when Haylee decides it's time to pack up and move back to California, you'll just wish her a safe journey and wave goodbye? Maybe you'll even be relieved, because then you can go back to spending your Saturday nights at Diggers', buying drinks for any pretty young thing who smiles at you. Because variety is the spice of life, right? A man would have to be a fool to settle down with one woman when there are so many who want to be with him."

"She's staying in Haven until after the babies are born."

"And then what?" Devin pressed.

"We haven't talked about anything beyond that," he admitted, ignoring the growing sense of unease inside him.

"Give her a reason to stay," his brother urged.

"I've already given her two."

Devin shook his head. "If you lose the most amazing woman you've ever known because you can't forgive your ex for her manipulations, then maybe you don't deserve her."

Haylee had no objection to Trevor going to Las Vegas with his brother. It felt strange being alone in his house, but she didn't worry about keeping herself busy. She had holiday baking to do, a couple of seasonal favorites to watch on the Hallmark Channel and *Beth & Amy*, a new release by her favorite author.

But still, keeping busy didn't keep her from missing him, so she decided to plan and prepare a special meal for his homecoming on Sunday. Nothing too fancy—she was still cautiously dipping her toe in the water when it came to actual cooking—but she found a fairly simple recipe for stir-fried chicken and vegetables and decided to give it a go.

Although The Trading Post wasn't too far to walk, she was still a California girl not just at heart but in her blood, so she opted to drive the short distance.

There was one light on Main Street, and of course it turned red as she approached. She applied her brakes carefully, in case the road was icy, and stopped at the line. She watched the green pickup truck in her rearview mirror as it stopped behind her, but the darker SUV-type vehicle was coming up fast behind it.

She heard the squeal of brakes as the SUV tried to stop, but it was too late.

Trevor didn't intend to wake her, but he needed to touch her, to reassure himself that she was okay. As he lifted his hand to lay it on top of hers, he saw that it was shaking—just like everything inside him.

Haylee's eyelids flickered, then opened.

"Hey," he said softly.

"Trevor? What are you doing here?"

"Where else should I be?"

"In Las Vegas with your brother."

"We turned around as soon as I got Sky's message that you were here."

"You didn't have to do that," she protested. "I'm fine. Sky should have told you that I was fine."

"She did," Trevor admitted. "But you were in a car accident and—" God, just saying it aloud made him feel sick.

"I wasn't really involved in the accident," she told him. "I was just at the end of a chain reaction caused by a distracted driver rear-ending the vehicle behind me."

"And yet you're at the urgent care clinic," he pointed out.

"The paramedics overreacted," she said. "They took one look at my belly and were worried that I was about to give birth on the side of the road and insisted I get checked out by a doctor."

"I'm glad they did," he said.

"But I'm fine," she said. "And our babies are fine."

"I'll believe it when the doctor springs you from this place."

"Consider her sprung," Dr. Foss said from the doorway.

"Really?" Haylee asked hopefully.

"Really," the clinic doctor confirmed.

"See?" she said to Trevor, just a little bit smugly.

"You might have some soreness and bruising from the seat belt," the doctor warned. "But there's nothing we can do about that. You can alternate hot and cold compresses on your back and neck, if you start to stiffen up. Otherwise just relax and let Mr. Blake take care of you."

"I can do that," Haylee said.

"I'll make sure of it," Trevor promised.

Despite her insistence that she could do it herself, he helped her dress. As he did so, he skimmed his hands over her torso, gently searching for any tender areas, and she rolled her eyes when he lingered in some of his favorite spots—the newest one being the round curve of her belly.

But aside from a red mark on her shoulder that would likely turn into a bruise in the next day or two, she didn't appear to be any the worse for wear. He helped her on with her coat, then her hat and mittens, reminding her that it was cold outside. "I know," she admitted. "That's why I was driving to the grocery store instead of walking."

"I should have been here for you," he said, feeling guilty that he wasn't and relieved that she hadn't been injured and terrified to think that she might have lost their babies—and he might have lost her.

"You're not responsible for what happened."

"I should have been here," he insisted, as they exited the clinic.

"You can't be with me every minute of every day."

"Says who?"

"Let me rephrase—I don't want you with me every minute of every day," she told him, softening the words with a smile. "You have to trust that I can take care of myself and our babies."

"How about every night?" he asked. "Can I be with you every night?"

Her smile widened. "I can't think of any reason that I'd object to that."

They were almost at the parking lot when she suddenly stopped, in the middle of the sidewalk, and tipped her head back. "Trevor…look."

He was looking—at her—as she held out her mittened hands, palms up, to catch the fluffy white flakes.

"Have you never seen snow before?" he asked, amused by her childlike wonder.

"Of course I've seen snow," she told him. "But it doesn't snow in Oakland. Ever." She watched a snowflake melt into the knitted fabric. "Actually, that's not true. I think it snowed once, maybe nine or ten years ago."

"We don't get a lot of snow here, either. Of course, this is the desert, so we don't get a lot of any kind of precipitation."

"Maybe the snow is a Christmas miracle," she suggested.

"Then it must be a year for miracles," he said, sliding his arms around her middle. "Because this is already the fourth."

"The fourth?" she echoed curiously.

He nodded. "You were the first." Then he splayed his hands on the curve of her belly. "Our son and daughter are the second and third, so this is the fourth."

Haylee felt her throat grow tight. "You really think our babies are a miracle?"

"Don't you?"

"I do," she agreed. "But I was afraid you'd think they were a mistake."

"Unplanned doesn't mean unwelcome," he said.

"That isn't quite what you were saying a few months ago."

"A few months ago, I was still reeling from the news of your pregnancy. And maybe afraid to let myself hope that this time…"

She placed her hands over his, a wordless gesture of understanding.

They stood silently for a moment, then Haylee felt a gentle nudge on the left side of her belly.

She heard his breath catch. "Was that…one of our babies?"

"It was. And that—" she said, when she felt another movement on the right side "—was the other one."

He turned her around then, so that she was facing him, and kissed her softly. "I love you, Haylee."

She hadn't expected to ever hear those words come from his lips, and though she desperately wanted to believe them now, she feared his declaration was an emotional reaction to the events of the day rather than a true reflection of his feelings.

"I'm sorry you were scared when you heard about the accident," she said cautiously. "But I think maybe you're twisting that fear into something else."

"I'm not," he denied. "Maybe I shouldn't have said the words for the first time standing outside of a medical clinic, but that doesn't make the feelings any less real. It's just that when I realized the truth of my feelings, I didn't want to wait a minute longer to share them with you.

"I'm not going to ask you to marry me again—not right now," he said. "Because I don't want you to think the words are tied up with expectations, but I want you to know that I'm sincere about wanting to be not just a father to our babies but a husband to you. A husband who will love and honor and cherish you every day of our life together. And when you're ready, I will happily get down on one knee and ask you to be my bride."

She didn't know how to respond, what to say. Then she heard the echo of her sister's words in her head—"take a leap"—and she did. "I love you, too." And it felt so good to finally release the feelings that she'd kept buried deep in her heart, she couldn't resist saying it again. "I love you, Trevor."

He kissed her then, on the grassy slope beside the urgent care clinic, while the snow continued to fall around them.

"And I want a Christmas Eve wedding," Haylee said, when he eased his mouth away from hers.

His brows lifted. "You want to get married?"

She nodded.

"*This* Christmas Eve?"

"Unless you think that's too soon," she said.

"Are you kidding? I would have married you three months ago," he reminded her.

"But you didn't love me three months ago."

"Or maybe I just didn't know that I did."

"Either way, I think we both needed some time to be sure what we wanted."

"Are you sure?"

"I'm sure," she said. "You made me believe that happily-ever-after is possible. You made me believe in us."

He touched his lips to hers again. "Then let's go home—we've got a wedding to plan."

Epilogue

Christmas Eve

"This was a ridiculous idea." Haylee frowned at her reflection in the full-length mirror. "I look like a beluga whale."

"You do not," Finley protested. "You look like a radiant bride."

"A very pregnant bride."

"Was your pregnancy supposed to be a secret?" her sister teased. "Because I doubt there's a hoop skirt anywhere in this world that would hide your babies bump, but I would have tried to find one for you."

"I just never imagined myself waddling down the aisle." She picked up her bouquet and held it in front of her, but the simple hand-tied arrangement of red roses with holly, ivy and mistletoe didn't hide anything, either. "Although truthfully, I'm not sure I ever imagined myself getting married at all."

"What are you talking about? Every little girl dreams about her wedding day," Finley said. "Doesn't she?"

"Maybe I did when I was a little girl," she acknowledged. "But as I grew up and rarely dated and never fell in love, I resigned myself to the fact that it wouldn't ever happen for me."

"And then you met Trevor."

Haylee smiled. "And then I met Trevor."

"And the Gilmores and Blakes drew battle lines."

She could laugh about it now—and did—but there had been a few moments when she'd wondered if the two families might come to blows. Most recently at the rehearsal dinner at The Home Station.

But her stepmother must have been a diplomat in a previous life, because somehow Colleen managed to smooth things over so that by the end of the night, Robert Gilmore and Elijah Blake were actually doing shots of whiskey together in honor of the happy couple.

"Seriously, though, I'm happy for you, sis." Finley's eyes filled with tears. "I'm going to miss you like crazy, but I'm happy for you."

"You're welcome to visit whenever you want."

"And I will," her sister promised. "But I'm still keeping Simon."

"I figured that out when we were in Oakland for Thanksgiving," she acknowledged. It didn't seem to matter to Simon that she was the one who'd taken him from the shelter; he'd quickly shifted his allegiance to the one who filled his food and water bowls every morning.

"Do you mind?" Finley asked.

She shook her head as a light knock sounded. "I know you'll take good care of one another."

"That better not be Trevor," Finley said, making her way to the door. "Because I told your soon-to-be husband, in no uncertain terms, that he was not allowed to see you before the ceremony."

She wrapped her hand around the knob and opened it just a crack, clearly prepared to send her future brother-in-law on his way if he'd dared to ignore her instructions.

"Oh," Finley said, and took a step back as she opened the door a little wider. "It's you."

Haylee stopped fussing with her flowers and glanced over her shoulder, wondering who it could be.

Then Sandra Burke stepped into the room.

"Mom." It was an effort to get the single word out through a throat that suddenly felt too tight.

"Look at you," Sandra murmured, her eyes shiny as she looked from one daughter to the other. "Both of you. My beautiful girls."

Haylee managed a wry smile. "Finley's beautiful. I'm pregnant."

"You're both beautiful," their mom insisted.

"I'll give you two a minute," Finley said, giving Sandra a quick hug before slipping through the still-open door and closing it firmly behind her.

"I didn't know you were coming," Haylee said, when her sister had gone.

"Your fiancé said he wanted it to be a surprise—

though I suspect he didn't say anything to you in case I didn't show up," Sandra admitted. "I missed far too many important events in your life.

"My fault, I know," she hastened to acknowledge. "But I couldn't let your wedding day be another one."

"I'm glad you're here," she said, surprised to realize it was true.

"Me, too," her mom said. Then, a little uncertainly, "Can I hug you—or will I wrinkle your dress?"

Haylee answered by stepping into her arms.

There had been a lot of debate and discussion about where Haylee and Trevor should get married. The bride's father thought the wedding should take place in her hometown; the groom's parents wanted to host it at Miners' Pass; Haylee had suggested the Silver Star, because it was where they'd first met; Trevor hadn't cared where the wedding happened—he just wanted Haylee to be his wife.

In the end, they'd decided to exchange vows in front of the Christmas tree they'd decorated together inside the home where they'd fallen in love.

"Nervous?" Devin asked, as he took his position beside his brother.

"Nope."

"Not even a little bit?"

Trevor shook his head. "I feel as if I've been waiting for this moment—for Haylee—my whole life."

"It seemed to take you that long to admit your feelings for her," his brother teased.

"True enough," he acknowledged. But now that he'd finally admitted what was in his heart, he'd vowed to tell her every day so that she'd never have cause to doubt his commitment to her and the family they were making together.

He wasn't nervous, but his heart did start to beat a little bit faster when the music started. Then Finley, dressed in festive red taffeta, made her way down the narrow aisle between the rows of chairs. A moment later, Haylee was there, looking more beautiful than he'd ever seen her, and his heart swelled with so much love for her, he felt as if his ribs might crack.

"Dear friends and family, we are gathered here today…"

The minister spoke about the sanctity of marriage and then guided the bride and groom through the exchange of vows, and then finally said, "I now pronounce you husband and wife."

He didn't conclude with an invitation for the newlyweds to kiss, but Trevor was prepared to take matters into his own hands. He pulled a sprig of a familiar green plant out of his pocket and held it over Haylee's head.

And smiling, he kissed his bride under the mistletoe.

* * * * *

COMING NEXT MONTH FROM

H HARLEQUIN

SPECIAL EDITION

Available December 1, 2020

#2803 A COWBOY'S CHRISTMAS CAROL
Montana Mavericks: What Happened to Beatrix?
by Brenda Harlen
Evan Cruise is haunted by his past and refuses to celebrate the festivities around him—until he meets Daphne Taylor. But when Daphne uncovers Evan's shocking family secret, it threatens to tear them apart. Will a little Christmas magic change everything?

#2804 A TEMPORARY CHRISTMAS ARRANGEMENT
The Bravos of Valentine Bay • by Christine Rimmer
Neither Harper Bravo nor Lincoln Stryker is planning to stay in Valentine Bay. But when Lincoln moves in next door and needs a hand with his niece and nephew, cash-strapped Harper can't help but step in. They make a deal: just during the holiday season, she'll nanny the kids while he works. But will love be enough to have them both changing their plans?

#2805 HIS LAST-CHANCE CHRISTMAS FAMILY
Welcome to Starlight • by Michelle Major
Brynn Hale has finally returned home to Starlight. She's ready for a fresh start for her son, and what better time for it than Christmas? Still, Nick Dunlap is the one connection to her past she can't let go of. Nick's not sure he deserves a chance with her now, but the magic of the season might make forgiveness—and love—a little bit easier for them both...

#2806 FOR THIS CHRISTMAS ONLY
Masterson, Texas • by Caro Carson
A chance encounter at the town's Yule log lighting leads Eli Taylor to invite Mallory Ames to stay with him. Which turns into asking her to be his fake girlfriend to show his siblings what a genuinely loving partnership looks like...just while they visit for the holidays. But will their lesson turn into something real for both of them?

#2807 A FIREHOUSE CHRISTMAS BABY
Lovestruck, Vermont • by Teri Wilson
After her dreams of motherhood were dashed, Felicity Hart is determined to make a fresh start in Lovestruck. Unfortunately, she has to work with firefighter Wade Ericson when a baby is abandoned at the firehouse. Then Felicity finds herself moving into Wade's house and using her foster-care training to care for the child, all just in time for Christmas.

#2808 A SOLDIER UNDER HER TREE
Sweet Briar Sweethearts • by Kathy Douglass
When her ex-fiancé shows up at her shop—engaged to her sister!—dress designer Hannah Carpenter doesn't know what to do. Especially when former fling Russell Danielson rides to the rescue, offering a fake relationship to foil her rude relations. The thing is, there's nothing fake about his kiss...

YOU CAN FIND MORE INFORMATION ON UPCOMING HARLEQUIN TITLES, FREE EXCERPTS AND MORE AT HARLEQUIN.COM.

HSECNM1120

"You sound like a counselor." The barest glimmer of a smile played around the edges of Brynn's mouth. "When did you get so smart, Chief Dunlap?"

"I was born this way. You never noticed before now because you were too dazzled by my good looks."

Her eyes went wide for a moment, and he wondered if he'd overstepped with the teasing. "I was dazzled by you. That part is true." She rolled her eyes. "But I guarantee you didn't show this kind of insight when we were younger."

He should make some funny comment back to her, keep the moment light. Instead, he let his gaze lower to her mouth as he took the soft ends of her hair between his fingers. "I might not have messed things up so badly if I had."

She drew in a sharp breath and he stepped away. This was not the time to spook her. "Come on, Brynn," he coaxed. "We both know it's not going to be good for anyone if you stay with your mom."

"She doesn't even want to meet Remi," Brynn told him, her full lips pressing into a thin line.

"Her loss," he said quietly. "All along it's been her loss. Say yes. Please."

She shifted and looked to where Tyler had disappeared with Kel. Without turning back to Nick, she nodded. "Yes," she said finally. "Thank you for the offer. I appreciate it and promise we won't disrupt your life." Now she did turn to him. "Very much, anyway," she added with a smile.

"Easy as pie," he said, ignoring the fact that his heart was beating as fast as if he'd just finished running a marathon.

Don't miss
His Last-Chance Christmas Family *by Michelle Major,*
available December 2020 wherever
Harlequin Special Edition books and ebooks are sold.

Harlequin.com

Get 4 FREE REWARDS!

We'll send you 2 FREE Books plus 2 FREE Mystery Gifts.

Harlequin Special Edition books relate to finding comfort and strength in the support of loved ones and enjoying the journey no matter what life throws your way.

FREE Value Over $20

YES! Please send me 2 FREE Harlequin Special Edition novels and my 2 FREE gifts (gifts are worth about $10 retail). After receiving them, if I don't wish to receive any more books, I can return the shipping statement marked "cancel." If I don't cancel, I will receive 6 brand-new novels every month and be billed just $4.99 per book in the U.S. or $5.74 per book in Canada. That's a savings of at least 12% off the cover price! It's quite a bargain! Shipping and handling is just 50¢ per book in the U.S. and $1.25 per book in Canada.* I understand that accepting the 2 free books and gifts places me under no obligation to buy anything. I can always return a shipment and cancel at any time. The free books and gifts are mine to keep no matter what I decide.

235/335 HDN GNMP

Name (please print)

Address   Apt. #

City   State/Province   Zip/Postal Code

Email: Please check this box ☐ if you would like to receive newsletters and promotional emails from Harlequin Enterprises ULC and its affiliates. You can unsubscribe anytime.

> ### Mail to the **Reader Service:**
> **IN U.S.A.:** P.O. Box 1341, Buffalo, NY 14240-8531
> **IN CANADA:** P.O. Box 603, Fort Erie, Ontario L2A 5X3

Want to try 2 free books from another series! Call 1-800-873-8635 or visit www.ReaderService.com.